Sweethaven
Twisted Tales of Familiar Faces
RJ Clark

M4L Publishing

Big Trouble in Little It'ly

Darkness descended on the village of Sweethaven. It arrived in the shape of a beast. The good Dr. Harold Friedman ducked down a shady-looking alley behind Lee's Cantonese and ran as fast and as far as his stumpy legs would take him. Out of the frying pan and into the fire. The Doc panted and gasped. The indulgent portions of spaghetti, eggplant marinara, and endless breadsticks he'd devoured like a hog slowed him down like an anvil tied around his waist. Hungry Harold never guessed it'd be his last meal.

He kept an eye over his shoulder, hoping he had ditched his stalker. The guy had been following Friedman ever since he left Giuseppe's Ristorante on Mott around ten. Midnight came and went forty-five minutes ago, and Friedman couldn't seem to shake the guy. He was like Friedman's shadow—everywhere the Doc turned, the shadow followed.

He didn't know who—or what—lurked in the dark, but the poor slob suspected. It didn't seem possible. The shadow died months ago. And yet, the Doc heard enough whispers to think maybe the death notice had been premature. But he didn't believe in ghosts.

Of the six scientists, only three remained breathing—including himself. And in a few moments, Friedman figured he'd be next in line to meet his maker. The moment of his reckoning had arrived.

Spotting a row of industrial dumpsters, he slid between them and sank to his feet, using them for cover. The brick wall felt good on his back. His legs were on fire. The last time he'd done any running was high school. Decent—never medaled—but nowadays he moved at a sloth's pace.

Just need a minute...to catch my br—

The Doc pressed harder against the wall as something metallic rolled down the alley. Maybe something fashioned out of tin. He didn't want to look, but forced himself in case the object turned out to be a bomb.

His head crept around the corner of a dumpster just as the object arrived at its destination—right in front of Friedman, who shrieked at the sight. The sound popped out of his mouth before he thought to stifle it. The thing staring from the dark, taunting him, was a rusty tin can with a faded label that read "SH Cannery. Spinach". It gave off a greenish glow and pulsed in rapid rhythm like a heartbeat.

A second later, the dumpsters flew down the alley one by one until the Doc lay exposed and vulnerable. The backstreet led to a dead end.

A massive hulking shadow appeared at the end of the alley. It covered the surrounding buildings as it strode toward the cowering Doc. Suddenly, a bright green glow cut through the dark. The Doc screamed as the one green eye locked on him.

"No! No, please!" The Doc covered his head and face with his hands. "It's not my fault! I didn't—"

Before he could blink, the hulking shadow with one green eye seized the Doc's throat and squeezed it with its meaty hands. The Doc's face turned a plum shade of purple as he kicked his legs into the air. The hulk held the Doc's thrashing body three feet off the ground. Not one of the Doc's futile kicks landed.

"I...didn't—"

A squeeze and a CRACK.

The Doc's neck snapped like a wishbone on Turkey Day. The hulk squeezed harder and harder. Its hands trembled as they gave the Doc's broken neck one last squeeze. The Doc's mouth fell open. A thin river of blood flowed onto the pavement.

Then, with an upward jerk, the Doc's head popped off. Blood fountained out of the Doc's twitching torso, exploding into the air like a volcano. A deep crimson covered years of neglected grime on the alley walls.

The hulk released its hand, and the Doc's body fell to the ground like a sack of rocks. It gave one final twitch before crumbling. The hulking shadow grabbed the Doc's head by its wet, matted hair. It tossed the Doc's dome into the air like a soccer ball and punted it down the alley, following it with its green eye until it disappeared.

The shadow laughed. Somewhere, a window shattered.

A woman screamed as a severed head crashed through her kitchen window and landed in a boiling pot of beef stew.

The Rent's Due

7:58 AM

My morning began with a BANG. Not a shot-in-the-back kind of bang, but a slamming of a door type of bang. My office door, to be precise. And only one creature can execute such a precise slam—an angry woman.

I didn't need eyes on the door to know the angry woman in question was my secretary and occasional bed mate, Dollface.

I'd recognize her brand of passive-aggressive fury anywhere.

And just in case you're wondering—no, I don't call Dollface "Dollface" as a term of endearment. That's her name, you see, because she's got an actual baby doll's face. Yeah, just like the plastic ones little girls use to play mommy. Kid you not. Nothing shocks me anymore. Not in Sweethaven.

I opened my eyes. They hurt even in the dim light. I ran my fingers through my hair and rubbed at my face, noting I was long overdue for a shave and shower. My hands sought my hat, which they quickly located. It lay crushed under my sleeping body. I fluffed my flat hat back into shape and heard—

Hurried footsteps shuffling through the front room, followed by the click of the desk lamp. The soft yellow light reflected on the frosted glass that separated my office from the front room.

The footsteps resumed. The pace quicker now, heading right for my office door.

The door flew open. I gave a small wave. It was met by a long, disapproving sigh.

"Aw, Jesus Christ, Chase," Dollface said. She folded her arms across her ample bosom and glared. "Did you 'forget' to pay the gas company again? The front room's colder than St. Paul in February."

She stomped over to the dusty radiator in the back corner of my office and kicked it several times. The clang rang louder than the noon bells at St. John's Cathedral. Dollface put one ear to the radiator, then touched the top of it with her hand.

"Well, you're lucky I brought a sweater, or this would've been the shortest day ever. Did you sleep on the couch again? How many nights is it now?"

"Good morning to you, too," I groaned.

It felt too early for words. Or was it too late?

"Good morning, Chase."

"Won't you be a doll, Dollface, and put the coffee on? Better make it strong. I'm gonna need all the help I can get today."

"You still not sleeping, Chase? Was it that dream again?" Dollface asked, referring to my recurring nightmare.

It started about six months ago, and I've dreamt it every night since.

I wiped the last bits of sleep from my eyes, yawned, and stretched. We both ignored the creaks and pops in my tired old bones as I stumbled to my feet.

Dollface resumed glaring.

"I'm not paying you to glare. I'm paying you to first make coffee. Second, answer the phone on the rare occasion it rings."

"It'd ring more if you paid Ma Bell."

I refused to be derailed.

"And, finally, this is the most important, sweet talk any Tom, Dick, Harry, or Jane that comes through the front door."

"There's only one problem with all that, Chase."

I knew what came next. Today, the rent was due, and I had a negative balance, and no credit left with Dollface.

"Yeah, and what's that?"

"You ain't paying me to do any of that stuff."

Her glare hardened. I didn't know a person *could* glare so hard.

I saw no point in denying it. Dollface hadn't seen a dime of pay in...well, a long while. I tucked a cigarette in my mouth and opened the blinds. Outside, another gray day.

"It's always raining. You ever notice, Dollface? It never stops raining in Sweethaven."

The rain pelted the windows. The drops sounded like pebbles on the glass.

"I can't remember the last time I saw the sun. Isn't it queer? Endless night."

I tossed the unlit cigarette into the trash bin beside my desk. Somehow, I didn't feel like smoking anymore. I felt like drinking. I needed something stronger than a plain cup of Colombian Gold. There was a bottle of moonshine that tasted like turpentine in my desk drawer, but it'd have to wait. Her old man drank himself to death. Liquor bottles triggered some hurt deep down inside of her. I'd put the kid through enough. I figured I'd spare her the sight of me getting loaded.

The surface of my desk and the trash bin looked like fraternal twins. They overflowed with crumbled papers, dirty day's old takeout containers, and newspapers so out of date their pages yellowed. I cleared a small patch on my desk and covered it with my forehead. The wood cooled my hot skin.

"You know what today is, don't you, Chase?"

"Still there, Dollface? I thought you were making—"

"Today is my last day working for you. Since I caught you two-timing me with that rat-faced bimbo—"

"The rat-faced bimbo is my landlady and be kind. She didn't choose her face any more than you did, doll."

Again, the answer is yes. My landlady had a genuine rat's face. Whiskers and all. God bless Sweethaven.

"I should have known better. I've seen you do it countless times with other women. Every time you're broke, which is always, and you owe some dame a dime, you charm 'em into your bed and expect it to cover your tab."

"Better than bouncing a check."

"You and a bounced check have a lot in common, Chase. You both ain't worth the paper you're printed on."

I didn't want to tell her I was more than a paper doll and she'd cut my heart with her shears, so I let her have her dig. I took it because I deserved it. At half-past four, she was walking out the front door and I didn't have any bread to make her stay.

"You've known me... how long, Dollface?"

She *hmphed*. "Too long. I shoulda cut you loose after the wax museum. Who takes a classy lady—"

"Oh, you're classy now, are you?"

"—a classy lady like *me* to a wax museum on a date? You're gonna die alone, Chase. Ah-lone."

"Yeah, maybe, Dollface. But I'll be happy. Single men live longer. That's a fact."

"Pooey!"

"You can't argue with science and can't argue with a woman. Single means there is zero chance of getting your brains rearranged by a frying-pan wielding wife who's upset because you forgot to get a loaf of bread on your way home after working a sixteen-hour day for the third day in a row."

"For once, you may be right, Chase. But you've got a knack for infuriating women. Married or not, let's face it. Your brains are gonna be on your kitchen cabinets sooner or later."

"Come on, Dollface. You knew who I was when we met. People don't change."

She flashed me that pitiful look women were born to wield. You know the one—the *I'm so disappointed in you* look. I've lost count of how many times it's been directed at me. Still, it stings harder than a slap to the face—depending on who is doing the slapping, I suppose.

"You know something, Chase? I bet you ain't never danced in the rain? Found joy in something so regular like rain. It's kinda sad, Chase. I'm sad for you."

I said nothing, nor did I blink or breathe. But I couldn't turn off the sweat. Dollface spotted it right away.

"You haven't. Ha! I knew it."

The disapproving look faded only to be replaced by the worst look of all—disgust.

"Today's the day, Chase. When I walk out that door, I ain't ever coming back. I mean it this time. Your number's up."

"I know, Dollface. I know. And I wish I could pay you everything I owe you and more, but I can't get blood from a stone."

"I wish you could, Chase. I really do. We coulda been somethin'. Like Bogie and Bacall."

I leaned back in my squeaky old office chair I'd rescued from the dump and hoped it'd survive one more day. Everything else around me was falling apart, so I figured the least the Universe could do for me was let my goddamned chair hold together just a little longer.

I couldn't think of anything else to say, so I went with—

"Yeah."

Simple and to the point. Our eyes met and held each other's gaze for a long, almost lovely moment. But I couldn't let myself linger there. Today was the day for closing doors, not opening cans of worms.

"Unless a paying client comes through that door before half-past four with a bag full of the green stuff, then I guess this is—"

Her voice trailed off as, on cue, the front door opened. We stared into the front room, eager to see who walked in. I think our jaws hit the floor at the same time. The sharpest dressed woman either of us had ever seen strolled into the front room like she owned the place. The dame could've stepped out of a show window of some fancy schmancy boutique. From the way she looked, I wondered if this was her first visit to the "other" side of town—the poor one. Home of the homeless, degenerate, destitute, and desperate. I fit in fine on this side of the tracks.

The mystery lady looked like money. Smelled like it too. Everything from her skin cream to the shampoo she used to wash her hair smelled like it cost more than what I should pay in rent for the office.

I gave her a quick once over. I tried not to make it obvious, but women always know when they've been x-rayed. I zeroed in on a strange-looking pendant that hung around her neck on a dull silver chain. I guessed it was a symbol of some kind. Religious, maybe? I couldn't place it, but I wasn't a believer. My faith lay in justice and the trigger of a .38 Special.

The pendant looked like tentacles forming an imperfect circle framing eyes of some kind. A fish or an octopus, maybe? The fisheyes caught a beam of gray light through the blinds and glowed green. They shimmered like small emeralds in the dull light.

The lady spoke and I sprang to attention in more ways than one.

"Detective Chase M. Down, I presume?"

"Depends on who's asking."

The dame reached into her pocketbook, and when she withdrew it, her hands were wrapped around a neat stack of what looked like brand-new fifty-dollar bills.

Dollface swooned. I thought she might go out cold seeing real-live money.

"Do you take cash?"

I tried to sound as cool as Jack Frost's balls.

"Lady, I'll take whatever you got to give. Come in. I'm Detective Chase."

Dick for Hire

Dollface couldn't contain her excitement. Her face beamed brighter than a pre-teen picking out her first titty trainer.

"I'll make some coffee," she said, taking her leave while inviting our new friend in.

The mystery woman took a slow, deliberate step into my office. It was almost as though she wanted to show off her shapely legs. This dame wanted to be seen. Taken in. Some dames are what we call "put together"—the sum of their parts appeals to the male gaze. And her parts would make a blind man blush.

The dame was trouble. Most are, but she was trouble with a capital T.

That's why I flew to her like a moth to a flame. I stole behind her and tapped the office door shut.

"Please, take a seat."

I motioned to the couch that doubled as my bed.

"That's an... interesting pendant. I don't recognize—"

"It's a *talisman*, not a pendant. It's a family heirloom."

She grimaced and gave the couch a pat down before lowering herself onto it.

"My mistake, missus?"

The dame hardened like clay in the sun.

"*MISS.*"

"Alright. Miss. That 'miss' come with a last name?"

She smiled without warmth. Pure theatre.

"Sorciere."

"Miss Sorciere," I parroted. "So, how can I help you?"

Dollface burst through the door, balancing a serving tray using both hands. The thing shook like my poor old Aunt Bertie. I figured the coffeepot and mugs bought a one-way ticket to the floor.

Miss Sorciere gave Dollface a sidelong glance but managed a polite nod when she presented her with a fresh cup of Colombian Gold.

"I'll cut to the chase, Chase," Sorciere said. She set down the untouched mug of mud. "I want to hire you. Today. Now."

I looked at Dollface. She looked at me. I turned my face into an expressionless mask.

"There are several other cases—"

Sorciere held up a hand, and like a good ol' whipped boy, I shut my mouth. Again, she reached into her bag and grabbed a handful of fifties. She smiled as she laid them out on the little table by the couch. A quick count of the bills told me she'd just put down an even grand without batting an eye.

"Here's your retainer. Will that do? I assume my case jumped to the top of the list? And whatever you normally collect per day, triple it. I promise you a sizable bonus if you close the case in a timely and... discreet manner."

Dollface's plastic eyes bulged. She made a strange chittering sound like a rabid rodent. I stepped back behind my desk, wondering what kind of chair I would buy with the money this dame was gonna pay me. The smell of the money had me aroused.

"You've got my attention."

"Do you mind if I smoke, Detective Chase?"

I retrieved the discarded cigarette from the trash bin and held it up.

"Not unless *you* mind."

Sorciere smiled. Dollface frowned.

"I thought you quit," Dollface whispered.

"Calms my nerves."

Sorciere smirked.

"Do I make you nervous, Detective Chase?"

She rummaged through her pocketbook and then pulled out a pack of imported cigarettes. I recognized the packaging at once—"Air Frais." *Fresh Air.* The smoke cost more than I earned in six months.

A second later, our cigarettes were lit, and the office was blanketed in a thick haze of smoke. Dollface coughed and waved the smoke from her face, but she kept her complaints to herself like a good girl.

"Have you heard of *The Raven's Claw*?" Sorciere asked. Her nostrils flared as two plumes of smoke exited.

"The dive bar behind St. Anthony's?"

"No. *The Raven's Claw* is my sailing vessel."

There was a hint of condescension in her voice, but I ignored it. It was her dime, and she had plenty to share, it seemed.

"Mighty queer name for a boat. Most sailors christen their boats after a gal pal or dear old mom."

"Then it's a good thing I'm not a sailor."

I took a drag and exhaled, eager to press her.

"If you're not a sailor or fisherman, then what are you?"

"A... financier."

"A financier?" Dollface asked.

"Yeah. She's the money," I explained.

Dollface nodded. Her cheeks flushed.

"Detective Chase is correct, my dear. Crudely put, but correct. I am 'the money'. I invest in projects I deem profitable. I use my money to make more money. Thanks to my investments, people have jobs and food on their table."

"Not a lot of entrepreneurial opportunities in Sweethaven other than making money off the labor of others."

Sorciere took a drag and held it in her lungs for close to a minute. Finally, she smiled and released it through her nose. The dame looked like one of those cartoon dragons.

"Would you rather the people live on the street and beg for the scraps?"

I laughed. "Look around. No scraps to spare here. Next week, I may be the one begging on your doorstep."

"Not if you take my case, Detective Chase. And if you play your cards right, you'll never work another day in your life. Either of you."

Dollface squeaked, but smothered it.

"So, what's the job, if I may ask?"

I prepared to hear the fine print. When something sounds too good to be true, there's fine print.

"You may ask, Detective Chase."

Sorciere reached into her pocketbook and produced what looked like a small photo. The kind you got from a ten cent photobooth. She held it up to Dollface. Their roles were clear—mistress and servant.

"Do you mind?" Sorciere said. "This couch is just so... comfortable."

Dollface knew the score and played her part as written. She took the photo and handed it to me.

"You're stalking me, Dollface. Put it in reverse. You're blocking the light."

"What light?" Dollface asked. She took in the gray skies through the blinds. After pouting for a bit, she made space—enough so she could still peek at the photo over my shoulder.

"Who's this?" I asked, looking at the photo of a generic sailor standing on a non-descript dock.

The sailor looked like every other sailor in Sweethaven except for one missing eye. An over-sized tobacco pipe dangled from his mouth. He looked on the thin side, but with some muscle tone. Next to the other sturdy sailors in Sweethaven, this guy would've been called a "pipsqueak".

"He, Detective Chase, is the job. I'm sorry. Would you be a dear?"

Sorciere held up the butt of her cigarette to Dollface as though she'd commanded a dog to fetch. Dollface obeyed like a good retriever. She tip-toed into the front room to dispose of the butt. I dumped mine into the rubbish bin.

"What's his story? Everyone's got a story."

I took a long, hard look at the woman sitting on my make-shift bed.

She was a woman with deep pockets. A woman who could settle my debt with Dollface, get the rent on the office paid up, and maybe have enough left for a new desk chair and couch. But something about her air changed since she waltzed into the office. It took a second for me to see it. The dame wore darkness like a fur coat.

I held up the photo of the one-eyed sailor.

"Let's start with the basics. This sailor got a name?"

I nodded to Dollface, the unspoken cue to take notes. My handwriting made Dr. Bartholomew's chicken scrawl look like it belonged on the wall of an art museum.

"His name," Sorciere began, stopping to wait for Dollface to open the pad and press pencil to paper. "His name is... Popeye."

"Pop...eye?" Dollface asked, looking up from her pad with a raised brow. "Is that one word or two?

"One. And yes. Popeye."

"So, Popeye the sailor guy. What do you want with him?" I asked, studying the photo again. I looked for more details. Something I missed the first time. Anything that could tell this guy's story, but nothing stood out. Beyond the ludicrous pipe and missing eye, the photo could have been a souvenir postcard sold at Mickey's Trading Post on Main Street.

"I want you, Detective Chase, to prove that Popeye the sailor is dead."

Never Trust a Raven

"Dead? What happened to the guy?"

"Lost at sea," Sorciere said.

It came out like a line. Rehearsed and unconvincing.

"Not like a sailor to get 'lost.'"

"Well, that one did. Fell into the sea while on board *The Raven's Claw*."

Ah, right. *The Raven's Claw*. I'd forgotten all about her boat.

"Fishing charter?"

Sorciere laughed at the mere suggestion she had anything to do with the trade, even though fish—and fishermen—were the bread and butter of Sweethaven.

"No. *The Raven's Claw* is a... recreational vessel."

"Recreational?"

"Yes, Detective Chase. Adventure on the high seas for the privileged—"

"Come on, lady. Just say rich. Why beat around the bush with flowery words?"

Something sour stirred in my belly.

"Yes. My clients are more upscale than..."

Sorciere gave the office a passing glance, as though she'd be struck blind if her eyes lingered on it too long. I doubted people like me and Dollface possessed the prerequisites for even being in the vicinity of Sorciere's vacation vessel—forget stepping foot on it.

I grabbed a second cigarette I spied under some fossilized Chinese fried rice and slid it between my lips. Dollface huffed as I gave it a light. I took a long drag and held the smoke in my lungs, buying a bit of time to consider my next play.

"It's funny how you high society types have no problem talking down to the rest of us not deemed worthy to eat the crumbs from your table, but you blush to say words like 'rich', 'well off', or 'affluent'."

My prospective client raised one of her thick, painted-on eyebrows.

"I'm not as simple a man as you think. I know a lot of fancy words. Comes in handy when someone acts as though I'm mud on the bottom of their heels."

I exhaled in Sorciere's direction. A small act of petty rebellion.

"No judgments, Detective. Honest. I just wanted to be clear about whom my business serves, and whom it does not."

It was about as empty an apology as they came, but I nodded. Really, I wanted to tell the dame to take a hike and look elsewhere for her dick. But I needed the money, and she knew it.

"Tell me about the trip."

"It was our maiden voyage, which is why it's frustrating. *The Raven's Claw* is aground until the matter is settled. I have another expedition booked. My clients are not used to hearing the word 'no'."

I'd bet my life the dame didn't hear it much either.

"Disappointment is all I know. What I wouldn't give to be on the winning side of things one time," I said. The cigarette no longer interested me. It was a distraction. "This maiden voyage... Popeye was part of the crew?"

"Yes."

"The destination?"

"Down the coast to the Cape."

"Cod?"

"Wrong direction. Cape Town. That's in—"

"South Africa. Right. I can read the atlas."

"Well, good for you, Detective Chase. Aren't you full of surprises."

I blew a long arm of smoke in Sorciere's direction as though it was a hand reaching out to touch her. Her expression said she got what I put down, or, in this case, exhaled.

"This next trip, the one you got pending release of your vessel. Back to South Africa?"

"No, the trip is a charter. The client owns a private island off Bermuda."

"Some guys have all the luck, don't they, Dollface?"

"More like some girls—"

"Listen, Detective Chase. My reputation is at stake. I need you to prove to the insurance company that Popeye is dead. Otherwise, the investigation will remain open, and *The Raven's Claw* will be grounded indefinitely."

I felt like there were a few puzzle pieces still missing. What I had didn't fit.

"What's the sticking point with the insurance guys?"

"There's no body."

"No body?"

"As I said, no. There's no body, so there's the rub."

"Forgive me in advance for asking this, but if there's no body, then how—"

"Do I know Popeye is dead?"

I nodded. My face said "obviously", although my mouth stayed zippered shut.

"Because no one could have survived a fall into those rough waters. If he didn't drown outright, then I imagine he smashed onto the rocks and the sharks got a little treat."

Dollface soured.

"I just lost my appetite."

"That's nature, Detective Chase. Pure Darwin."

I thought about the war. I survived the fighting, but I was not the fittest. I just got lucky. Sometimes in life, that's all it takes to survive—luck. Well, luck and a loaded .38.

"My vessel needs to be on the water in three days."

Dollface dropped her pencil. She picked it up in a hurry, as if her birth control pills had spilled out of her bag onto the church floor in the middle of Easter mass.

"I beg your pardon?"

Sorciere hardened. "You heard me. Three days. And not a second longer."

"Get real, lady. Even your basic missing person case takes at least a week to investigate, and longer to close. And this isn't your basic find or retrieve."

"How so?

"The distance, for one. South Africa ain't exactly one town over."

"Poppycock. I'll give you a list of names. People who will give you what you need to close this case, on paper, to everyone's satisfaction."

"Who needs to be satisfied?"

"The only one who matters is Mr. Ronald J. Moser. The insurance investigator at Hong and Dong and Co."

I hoped Dollface put that name down in our little black book. With my brain cells popping faster than a birthday balloon in a needle factory, I'd end up at Ding-Dong's—home of the longest, and only, all-beef burlesque show.

"So, it doesn't matter if the guy's even dead or not. You just need someone to declare it on the official record, is that right? If he's 'dead', you're cleared and go back to vacationing with the rich and famous."

Sorciere sighed and then took a long breath.

"He's dead. This is your chance to get out. Your winning ticket, Detective Chase. And if you close this case for me in three days or less, I will reward you beyond your wildest dreams."

This was her polite way of saying that the money would make me better. All better. Having money like that wouldn't just open doors that had previously been closed, but install them, too, in places where no doors previously existed.

"How many other private dicks did you tempt with that same shiny apple before you waltzed into my office?"

Sorciere looked surprised. I've been underestimated before. It goes with the job. But the look I get when I turn the tables? I live for it.

"You've got me there, Detective Chase. There aren't enough dicks in Sweethaven."

"You ain't kidding," Dollface mumbled.

Sorciere smiled. A little warmer this time.

"To be blunt, I've run out of both dicks and time. You're my last and only hope. I need *The Raven's Claw* cleared to leave port in seventy-two hours."

"Have you considered you might be wrong? Maybe he's still out there somewhere?"

"I'm never wrong."

"Sure, you say he's not. But if he is... what does that mean for me?"

"Dead or alive, I will see to it you get everything you deserve and more. Think of what you can do with all that money."

Just then, I understood how the snake conned Eve into taking a bite of the forbidden fruit. I looked at Dollface. Her eyes said *no, it's a fool's bet, Chase.* But I owed her. More than the money. I had to close out our tab, and this broad was my golden ticket.

I didn't know how to tell Dollface I was doing this for HER. So at least one of us would make it out of Sweethaven. I prayed she still trusted me for one last mystery.

And that's why it all happened the way it happened. My noble intentions. Funny how even when you do something for the right reasons, it can still go bad.

But we'll come to that.

Dollface sucked in her breath as I turned to Sorciere and said—

"Lady, you just bought yourself one helluva dick."

Love Walks In

9:52 AM

Sorciere slipped me a fancy embossed card with her addresses and a phone number. She lived high on the hill—Rattle Snake Hill—looking down on us common folks. I wondered what she saw up there, perched in her nest.

She also gave me the name of the other crew members who worked on *The Raven's Claw* alongside Popeye. A skeleton crew for the supposed size of the vessel. I asked myself if that was deliberate or if *The Raven's Claw* was a ghost ship?

Sailors won't work on a ghost ship. It's a blacklist. They call them "ghost ships" because there's no crew to pilot them. The usual reason? Getting stiffed on pay. Did Sorciere welch on her crew?

I freshened up at the sink in my bathroom. My teeth desperately needed a brushing, and my hair whipped back into place. I was drying my hands on a not-so-fresh towel when Dollface stepped into my office.

"Chase?"

"In here."

She took a few steps closer to the can and stopped. I'd lived alone so long that I'd gotten used to not closing the bathroom door while I did my business. And much to her horror, Dollface wandered into my office frequently while I conducted said business.

"Chase, there's a woman here to see you."

What were the odds? No one punched my dance card in over a month, and now in a single morning, two dames tapped my shoulder for a swing. I didn't like it.

"She says she's Popeye's girl."

That got my attention. I threw the towel aside, wiping the last traces of soapy suds onto my slacks, and stepped into the office to greet my latest guest.

She was a tall, slender gal dressed in a washed-out flapper skirt that went down to her ankles. On top, she wore a faded red long-sleeved blouse with dingy white trim. Several long threads poked out like little snakes from small holes in the fabric. Her black hair was pulled back in a tight ponytail, but much of it had broken free, giving her an unkempt look.

The dame had the roundest, darkest eyes I'd ever seen. Other than the bits of white, I couldn't make out if her eyes were blue, green, or gray. If there had been no whites in them, I would have thought she was missing both eyes—unlike her fella, Popeye, who lacked the one.

I held out a hand. She stared at it for a long, uncomfortable minute. It looked as though the dame was making sure there were no festering boils on my skin. Satisfied, she took my hand, and we shook. Her grip felt loose and weak. I wondered if I'd break her bones if I squeezed any harder.

"Chase, I'd like you to meet Miss Oyl."

"Please," the dame said, separating our hands and studying her own, as if expecting something to sprout after making contact with mine. "Call me Olive."

Olive had a squeaky, high-pitched voice. It was one of those voices that grated on your nerves after a while, like fingernails on a schoolhouse blackboard. I wondered how Popeye put up with it, or maybe he'd taken a swan dive into the sea to escape it.

"Okay, Olive. Why don't you take a seat and tell me everything?"

I hoped her tale was a short one, otherwise I might be the one taking a dive into the sea. Sorciere had me on the clock, and it was ticking fast. Lucky for me, Olive's story was short and sweet, kind of like Dollface. But I'd never tell her that. It'd inflate her already oversized head.

The sweet part of her story was the romance with her fella. It sounded like they were in love, at least I believed Miss Oyl loved the one-eyed sailor. Only time would reveal if the feeling was reciprocated. The answer might explain the sailor's absence. Frying pan to the head. Just a fact.

She related Popeye was a sailor and an explorer with a knack for finding lost treasures and artifacts.

"He has a sixth sense for it," Olive said. Her eyes glazed over. And for an instant, Miss Oyl went a million miles away.

"Or the nose of a bloodhound," Dollface said to lighten the mood and bring Olive back to the office.

Olive stared at her third-rate shoes. "Popeye thought if he found the right treasure, it would be enough to get out of Sweethaven and start our life together somewhere else. Somewhere less…"

"Dreary," I offered.

She nodded.

"I know what you mean. It rains all the time now. You notice that?"

Olive gave no response. The way she stared off into nothing, I thought she'd checked out on me.

"Tell me, Miss Oyl."

The name roused her from her daydream.

"Sorry. Tell me, Olive."

Her face eased. I noticed then she was an attractive woman, in her own way. Her face would probably never be on the cover of a fashion rag, but she was no Plain Jane. She wore her heart on her sleeve, but who could fault her for being in love? Certainly not me when the closest I got to the bug was Dollface, and that hadn't ended well for either of us.

My recurring dream snuck back into my head. It came every night now. A village swallowed by mist. Something rising out of the sea. Relentless rain. This dark version of Sweethaven kept me awake on my couch, and now the dream haunted my waking hours as well.

Studying Olive, with the dark dream fresh in my head, I knew they were connected—my dream, *The Raven's Claw*, and Miss Olive Oyl—but I couldn't figure out how. Not yet.

"Tell me, Olive. Do you dream much?"

Crime Pays

10:11 AM

Popeye was a popular guy. Two dames wanted the one-eyed sailor located ASAP. One needed him dead on paper for her livelihood, and the other wanted the sailor still among the living to mend her broken heart.

Sorciere didn't care. Dead or alive, made no difference to her. The dame just wanted to sail off into the sunset with her rich pals. She'd forget the guy's name as soon as the harbormaster cleared her ship.

But Miss Oyl? Olive was the heart of the case. And I didn't have the heart to take her money. The dame looked like she needed it more than me. And I figured Sorciere's retainer covered Olive's fee—and then some. Now I just had to hope *Mizz* Sorciere was on the level, and I saw the rest of the dough she'd dangled before me.

I stepped out from under the awning and onto the street. The rain let up enough to move about without an umbrella. A thick blanket of green mist hung over the streets. If I didn't know any better, I'd have sworn on a stack of *Field & Stream* that the mist glowed. I brushed it off as a trick of the light, but looking back, I should have known better. There isn't any light in Sweethaven.

I looked over the list of names Sorciere provided, deciding to start on the other end of the village, working my way back. Tucking the list into my coat pocket, I set off into the rain.

The village slept. The streets were too quiet for a weekday morning. I didn't like that one bit. Quiet unnerved me. I felt like the Omega Man. The last guy standing in Sweethaven.

Last guy or not, I felt eyes on me. Unseen eyes, watching from the shadows. Tracked like a deer. I brushed it off and as I crossed the street. Tommy, our paper boy, barreled into me. Even though the kid nearly knocked me onto my keister, I had to admit I was relieved to see another face.

"Oh, sorry, Mr. Down. Didn't see ya there!"

"Nothing's broken. I think I'll live. Where's the fire, Tommy?"

"I got a short stack—"

In paper boy lingo, his allotted papers were light.

"I had to go to the office to get more. Fourth time this month. Who'd wanna steal that many papers? The *Sweethaven Sun*, no less!"

The *Sun* wasn't worth the paper it was printed on.

"That IS a mystery, kid."

I fished a couple of coins out of my pocket and tossed them to Tommy. His eyes popped open as he counted the coins in his hand. It wasn't much, but enough to put something in the kid's belly for the day. Something the newsie's father didn't care to do.

"Keep the change, kid."

"Thanks, Mr. Down. You're alright."

The kid handed over a copy of our illustrious local rag and darted down the street. He looked over his shoulder and gave a small wave. I returned it, and as I watched him disappear into the mist, I wondered who'd wanna steal his papers. The boys paid out of their own pockets when their stacks turned up short. It was quite the racket old Pete Peterson, the editor and chief buffoon, had going.

I wanted to help the kid. Everyone in Sweethaven needed help these days, and thanks to Sorciere, I could dole a little out. I made a note to investigate Tommy's dilemma.

I turned my gaze to Peterson's rag and zeroed in on the headline—

"HEADLESS SCIENTIST FOUND DEAD!"

Without a head, one would assume the guy's dead. Cracker-jack writing, Peterson.

I noted the sub-heading—

"THAT MAKES FOUR."

Four? How'd I miss those headlines?

I stuffed the paper into the front pocket of my raincoat. With any luck, there'd be time to read the rag later. I got the feeling from Sorciere that the case would be closed in record book time. Go through the motions. Talk to a few witnesses, listen to tales of woe, do a little figuring, and put my stamp on it to get all that green stuff.

Easy money. Only, there's no such thing.

I turned to make my way to the first address on Sorciere's list, but I didn't get far. The next thing I knew, I found myself sandwiched between two slabs of prime Italian beef. I shoulda been more careful, but you live, you learn. The goons each grabbed an arm and hoisted me up like a chicken.

"Hey, Chase. Remember us," Goon Number One, aka Vinnie Vespa, said.

"Who could forget a face like that?"

"Ouch, Chase. You hurtin' our feelin's. You wouldn't wanna do that now—"

Goon Number Two, aka Nicky Gigante, twisted my arm.

"Would ya?"

"Okay, okay. Sorry, fellas. You mind?"

Nicky released my arm. I made a note to grab some aspirin later.

"Let's go for a little ride. The Boss wants to see you."

The Boss—Don Anthony Santino III, head of the Santino crime family. One of the five 'families' in our quaint little village.

"Listen, boys. I'm up to my neck in cases right now. Rain check?"

I heard the click of a revolver and knew one of Santino's goons had the barrel on me. I'd end up with a few holes before I got to my .38.

"It's not a request, smart mouth. Nicky, how did Mr. Santino put it?"

Nicky laughed.

"Bring me dat lousy private dick today, or someone's gonna be payin' Mr. Jimmy a visit. Permanent-like."

Nicky did a solid impression of the old Don. I would have applauded, but the goons still had me hoisted up by my arms.

"Mr. Jimmy, huh? Must be serious."

Nicky flashed a toothy smile. "Dead serious, Chase."

Every snitch and dick in Sweethaven knew the legend of Jimmy Falcone. Caught red-handed with his... in Santino's first wife's... Poor guy ran to the Feds to turn state's evidence on his former boss, and his former lover's husband. And the rest is urban legend. Wife numero uno went on "an extended holiday" in Florence, Santino married wife number two—a newer model. And now Mr. Jimmy sleeps at the bottom of the sea in a fitted pair of cement shoes.

"Yeah, I hear Mr. Jimmy's not a real talker these days. Fish food. You wouldn't want that for me, would you, fellas? Come on. It's me. Chase."

Nicky grinned, no doubt picturing a piranha nibbling at my nose.

"Say, Vin. Let's just tell the old don we couldn't locate this dick and let the fish at him. They're real hungry this time of year. It's matin' season, right?"

"You do that, and you'll be packing your bags for a one-way trip to Florence."

The smile left Nicky's droopy, round face.

"It's settled. Let's not keep Mr. Santino waiting then, shall we, fellas?"

A four-door black sedan with the darkest tinted windows curbed a wheel.

Joey "The Wheel" Nitti, one of Santino's drivers, failed his driving test so many times the DMV blacklisted him from ever getting a license. That didn't stop him from becoming one of Santino's most trusted employees. And there wasn't a cop in Sweethaven brave enough to write The Wheel a ticket.

Vinnie opened the back door and Nicky slid in. Next came my turn. Vinnie pocketed my .38 and then shoe-horned me in beside Nicky before climbing in. I felt like a slice of cheese sandwiched between two all-beef burgers. Vinnie pulled the door shut, and The Wheel put the sedan in reverse. Then, with a screech, we drove through the village, heading straight for the mansion of Anthony Santino.

Few stepped inside the mobster's palace, and of the ones who did, even fewer lived to talk about it. I considered my odds and shook my head. More of my rotten luck—I end up at the bottom of the sea right when my ship came sailing in. *The Raven's Claw.*

I didn't make it this far to end up fish chow. One way or another, I was walking out of Santino's home—either crawling or on my two feet.

The Offer You Can't Refuse

10:29 AM

Santino's palatial pad exceeded my expectations. Crime paid well. I was on the wrong side of things. Struggling for every nickel and dime. Following the rules like a good boy. And guys like Santino did as they pleased and swam in dough. The Universe had a funny sense of humor.

Santino's goons led me on a brisk tour of the first floor. Something told me I wouldn't see much more of the mobster's digs. The place looked like a museum. Gaudy statues of Catholic saints and the Virgin sat in glass display cases, lit from above by spotlights so their light looked heaven sent. Plastic covered the furniture. In the corner of the great room, a full bar tempted.

My pals Nicky and Vinnie hurried me through a door in the kitchen. It led to the sprawling backyard, where larger gaudy statues decorated every nook and cranny of the green space. The place looked like a drunken decorator emptied his warehouse and stuck every bit of kitsch in Santino's yard.

A colossal pool, as ornate as the rest of the yard, made its home in the center of the Santino preserve for tacky nicknacks. The pool looked twice the size of the one at the Y. Santino swam solo. He tipped a full old-fashioned glass to his lips as he sunned himself on a gigantic float—even though no sun shone in the sky above Sweethaven.

Santino looked up from behind his fashionable sunglasses. His eyes locked in on me. My pace slowed, despite the insistent shove I received from the Mafia Mario Brothers. Santino smiled and waved. I wanted to feel relieved, but the gesture only fed my anxiety.

"My good friend, Detective Chase M. Down," Santino yelled from his floating couch. "Drink?"

Vinnie pushed at my back so hard that I almost fell into the pool. I shot him a scowl over my shoulder.

"Hey, Mr. Santino. No, thanks. I'm on the clock."

"For real? I've never known a dick dat didn't like to get wet."

"Maybe that's why they're out of business."

Santino laughed.

"Yeah, from what I'm hearin', you ain't exactly flush, Chase."

Vinnie snickered in my ear.

"Good news travels fast, I see, Santino."

The mobster winked.

"Dat's all, fellas. I'll call if I need you, but I t'ink the good dick will be on his best behavior. Not like last time we came face to face. Right, Detective?"

"Your goon pulled a gun."

"And you plugged him right between da eyes. It was a fair hit, which is why you're still breathin', Chase."

I didn't doubt Santino. The guy was honest for a crook.

"Take a walk, fellas."

Vinnie sighed but did as told. Nicky trailed hot on Vinnie's penny loafers. The latter gave one last look over his thick shoulder.

"Call if you need me, sir."

Santino raised his glass.

"I'll do just dat, Nicky. Thank you."

A second later, the goons were gone, and I found myself alone with one of the most vicious killers to ever walk the streets of Sweethaven. And without my .38, I didn't like my odds. I bet Santino had a piece stashed on that raft or tucked down his baggy swim trunks.

"Meatheads. It's so hard to find good help t'ese days. Wouldn't you agree, Chase? You still got dat pretty doll working for you?"

"I do, Mr. Santino."

"You payin' her?"

I looked away.

"As I t'ought. Times are tight in our little village, no? Hard-working men begging on street corners. Vagrants. Drunks. Da place has gone to hell, Chase."

For once, I agreed with Santino. I made a note to check if hell froze over.

"Let me ask you somethin', Chase."

Santino hopped off the raft, not spilling a drop from his glass. The sunglasses didn't fare as well. I watched as they sank to the bottom. Santino made his way to the stairs and climbed out of the pool.

He set the glass on a table that sat at the end of a long row of sunning loungers.

"You read that waste of paper Peterson pretends is a legit newspaper?" Santino asked as he grabbed a fresh towel from a brass cart and dried off. A stocked matching gold mini bar sat beside the cart.

"Only when forced, sir."

"Ha, good man. I knew I liked you for a reason, Chase. Come, sit."

Santino motioned to a decadent solid gold patio set. I imagined on a sunny day the table glistened. He took his place like a king at the end of the long table and took a drink from his glass.

I pulled out a chair and sat beside Santino.

"You read that rag lately?"

I pulled today's edition out of my pocket.

"I haven't read it yet. Skimmed the front page."

Santino laughed.

"'Headless Doctor Found Dead'. Can you believe what passes for good journalism t'ese days? Mamma Mia!"

Santino emptied the last of the liquor into his mouth. A bit of the brown stuff dripped down his chin and got lost in a forest of chest hair. He held up the empty glass.

"You sure I can't tempt you, Chase?"

"I'm good, Mr. Santino."

"Suit yourself. Anyways, as I was sayin'. You notice any mention of me or my, shall I say, competitors on the pages of dat rag?"

I thought back. The number of pages between the covers had dwindled to a dozen and change in recent months. A sign of the times. But among feel-good stories about finding lost pets, announcing the winner of the Sweethaven Elementary Spelling Bee, and the latest obituaries, I couldn't recall a single mention of the dons.

"No, can't say I have."

Santino sauntered to the mini-bar and refilled his glass. He threw a handful of ice cubes in for good measure.

"Don't you t'ink dat's a bit... odd? Considering the circumstances?"

Santino took a sip as he crossed back to the table.

"I'm sorry, Mr. Santino. You left me on the dock and sailed off without me. What circumstances?"

Had some higher-up gotten pinched and flipped? A hit? No bells rang in my head, but the crickets chirped.

"Let me set the record straight."

Santino's face soured. He downed the rest of the liquor and set down the glass.

"I'm da only one left, Chase. Can you believe it? Da very last one."

Chirp. Chirp. Chirp.

"I'm sorry, Mr. Santino. I have no—"

"De're dead, Chase. The other dons. Dead!"

The news hit me like a slug to the shoulder. News like that should've made the front page.

"I'm the last don standing, Chase. Dat means I'm next."

"No disrespect, Mr. Santino, but how do you know they're dead? I haven't heard—"

"No, you haven't, have you? Don't you t'ink dat's odd, Chase?"

"Well, I think news like that, if it were true, would be headline material. Peterson doesn't know much, but he knows a good HEAD-line."

Santino stared at me for a second, then burst into laughter.

"HEAD-line! You're too much, Chase. I always say dat 'bout you. You gotta good head on your shoulders."

He hadn't meant for the pun, which only increased his laughter. I gave a small smile and waited for the moment to pass.

"As I was sayin', I know de're dead because their crews cleared out. Skipped town. Took nothing with dem, either. No guns. No booze. No money. Hell, dey even ditched their broads. Just up and vanished like dat writer. Pierce? Bierce? I don't know."

"And the dons?"

"Gone."

"What do you mean, gone? Gone where?"

Santino closed his eyes and moved his hands into the prayer position.

"Gone to the great gelato factory in the sky."

He opened his eyes and laughed like a schoolboy in sex-ed.

"They're just gone, Chase. Haven't you noticed t'ings have gotten a bit odd in our little village? Somet'ing ain't right."

I knew what Santino meant. *Endless night.* A sickness walked the streets of Sweethaven.

"Yeah, with the dons out of commission, this whole town is on the market. And I want it, Chase. It's mine. I earned it. But first, I need to know what happened to the competition. And dat's the mystery you're going to solve for me."

I blinked and then leaned in.

"Excuse me?"

Santino sat back and tucked his hands behind his head.

"Oh, I know you heard me, Chase. You got dem bat ears. Sonar, isn't it? You hear t'ings miles away."

Thanks to the pop of a gun inches from my face, I'd lost most of my super-hearing—although I still picked up more than your average Joe. I saw no need to clue in Santino.

"I, Anthony Salvatore Santino III, want you, Detective Chase M. Down, to find out what happened to Don Giovanni, Don Lemone, Don Perry Gon, and Don Pedro."

"Mr. Santino—"

"And I need you to do dis for me before the same thing dat happened to dem, happens to me, capisce?"

I understood all too well. Either I do this for him, or me and Mr. Jimmy were gonna be neighbors.

"I know what you usually collect for jobs like dis, and I'm prepared to do better dan dat. A lot better. Dis is my life I'm talking about, Chase. And dat is worth a lot of cheddar to me. And plenty for you, too."

Decisions, Decisions

11:04 AM

Not even noon and already I was in the thick of it. On one hand, I had the two dames—the financier and the gal-pal. And on the other, the paperboy and the mobster. Right there in the middle... me.

The rain came down in buckets. My raincoat did little to keep me dry. I pictured Santino, sipping cocktails in his pool in the hard rain. I smiled at the thought and went on my way. Destination—Flo's Coffee Shop. I needed a hit, and Flo made the best cup o' joe in Sweethaven.

Despite the downpour, the streets of Sweethaven teemed with activity. And life. Not hustling and bustling, but the town didn't look six feet under anymore. I took the Sunday driver's route to Flo's shop. I needed to think and clear my head, but also, I wanted to get a look at the docks. And the sailors. Sniff around.

I walked several blocks, nodding at passersby. The docks came into view. And then I stopped dead. How had I missed it? It stared me in the face. Literally. The people. The people of Sweethaven... changed. And some were still changing. From human to something other. Some looked to be human-fish hybrids, and others... I couldn't guess.

Occasional oddities were nothing new to Sweethaven. Dollface. Ratface. But this felt different. This metamorphosis was happening on a grand scale. Everyone appeared affected. Or *infected*.

As I hit the docks, I noted the sailors were most affected. Twisted bodies. Fin-like appendages. Razor-sharp teeth. Saucer-sized cloudy black eyes. Uneven lines of scales up and down the length of their backs. Shimmering green dorsal fins. Exaggerated, open-mouthed breathing. Just like fish in the water.

The water. Green sea water.

I took it all in. The scope of it. And I wondered what, if anything, Popeye, Sorciere, Olive, Jimmy the paper boy, and Santino had to do with it. I decided I would find out. Cure Sweethaven of its sickness once and for all. Time to see if one man CAN make a difference.

Joe to the Rescue!

11:34 AM

I arrived at Flo's Coffee Shop half an hour later. I lingered at the docks longer than I'd planned, but I wanted to see it all. And I got an eyeful. The stuff of nightmares. The variety of fish-people walking the streets of Sweethaven told me I had little time to set things right before our village turned into an over-sized aquarium for freakish fish.

Three days.

I gave Flo my order—cup o' joe and black toast with butter—and made my way to the bathroom. Water dripped from every part of me. I guess I looked like a squirrel that drowned in a swimming pool because Flo dispensed with the small talk. A kindness I noted to thank the gal for later. I might have imagined it, but I could've sworn since yesterday old Flo's eyes had lost their color, and her mouth opened and closed with every breath.

There must've been a towel shortage in Sweethaven because the shop's bathroom stocked only two child-sized hand towels—both had seen better days. I dried myself off as best as one could with the inadequate tools on hand. The rain had washed away some of my grime.

I slid back into my booth in the corner and took a hit of liquid caffeine, feeling my systems turn on at the first drop. I needed my brain cells in peak form for the coming seventy-two hours.

"Flo, honey?"

The walrus-sized, fishy waitress's head appeared at the kitchen pass-through. She opened her mouth and closed it again as she took several shallow breaths. Two sets of pearly-white pointy teeth glistened in the light of the food warmer as Flo smiled.

"Yes, d-d-dear?"

"I think you'd better put on a pot. I'm gonna need it."

"Comin' right up!"

Her head sank below the pass-through as though she was standing on a movable platform. For the first time in a dozen years, I was relieved to see Flo vanish.

That's when I knew I'd made the right decision. Sweethaven had been good to me, kinder than some others, and I figured this settled my account.

First stop: the dockmaster's office to get a look at *The Raven's Claw* manifest.

Manifest Destiny

I found the harbormaster's office deserted and locked up tighter than the communion wine at Saint Francis. Gotta watch Father Angus around wine. I knocked on the door, but nothing stirred inside. A thick layer of muck covered the glass on the front windows, so I went around the back of the building to give the back ones a look.

Turned out that'd been a smart move. A broken windowpane gave me the visual access I needed. I peered through the broken glass into the dark, dank office. I spied the usual suspects—a couple of desks, mismatched chairs, file cabinets. Nothing out of the ordinary.

But then I caught a noseful of something unusual. It smelled like rotten eggs and decay. Not a pleasant combo. I pulled my nose out of there and fought back the urge to regurgitate my toast.

I stepped away from the window and was about to go back around to the front when something else caught my eye. A faint green light pulsing somewhere inside the harbormaster's office. The next room, maybe. Someone, or some*thing*, was in there.

I removed my raincoat and fashioned it into a flat square, which I then used to muffle the sound of me breaking the rest of the glass. It did the job, but with more noise than I would've liked. I used the folded coat to brush away the broken bits on the sill, then climbed through.

As soon as my feet touched the floor, I pulled the coat up to my nose to stave off the noxious smell. Inside, the pungent fish odor did not complement the scent of rotten eggs. I crept through the back room, careful to use a light step. I wanted the element of surprise, if I still had it after smashing the broken window.

Even in the dark, I saw there was nothing useful for me there. A nest of spiders called the filing cabinets home, otherwise they were empty. I got the feeling the harbormaster's office was gonna be a bust, but I continued my search just in case.

A bathroom sat adjacent to the back office. I cracked the door open a sliver to peek inside and see if the foul odor originated there. But I didn't catch a whiff of anything unexpected. The shitbox reeked with a tangy funk, just like the men's room at Union Square station.

I stepped into the hall and moved down a few feet to the front office—the spot where both the smell was at its worst and the glow shone the brightest. About to take another step, a stabbing pain tore through my back. I bit my tongue to stay quiet as I melted onto the floor.

Instinct told me to reach for my .38.

I did and slammed my fist into the floor. Santino's goons never returned my piece. I made a note to circle back and retrieve it. Next, I reached around to my back and checked for any sign of injury—like blood or a knife handle sticking out of a shoulder blade.

I felt nothing.

At first.

I pressed harder into my back, just to be sure. And damn.

Something WAS there, under my shirt.

Hard and scaly.

It felt like... gills.

Fish gills.

Ch-Ch-Changes

1:08 PM

I stared at my reflection, horrified by the sight of me. Gills. Freakin'… gills. I looked like a monster. A sea monster from a bad sci-fi movie. I doubted ol' Sam Hammett carried a cream at Dashiell's Drugs for the stuff coming out of my back.

I wondered how long until I looked like the hybrid sailors down at the dock. They'd grown bigger in just the minute I'd been inspecting my new body parts. The gills pressed against my shirt, ready to punch a hole right through the thin material.

Like I said, human oddities were nothing new in Sweethaven. But now, it appeared everyone had been infected by some unseen sickness—whether or not they showed signs. The gills on my back served as proof that the pace and rate of infection accelerated. In another couple of days, it'd spread to everyone.

Three days.

For now, I'd need a bigger, baggier raincoat to keep my gills for my eyes only.

Meanwhile, the clock ticked.

Less than sixty-seven hours to get Popeye the sailor guy declared dead or find the guy hiding out in a hostel on the coast. Santino and the dons. Who knew how long the don had left. A day? Two? Hours? Minutes?

And how long before I grew webbed feet and claws, or stalked women as they swam through my deep, dark sea?

Instinct told me my time, the don's time, and Sorciere's time were all the same. I only had to figure out how long before the last sands dropped in the hourglass.

I couldn't do a thing about my fish problem, so I crept toward the front room. Every floorboard creaked and groaned under my weight.

How many pounds did the gills add to my mass?

So much for the quiet approach.

I rounded the corner, unsure what or who I'd find in the front office. I could kick myself for leaving my piece with Santino's goons. Terrible odds going into a dark room in a building I had broken into twenty minutes ago.

But I found the room deserted. And in shambles. Every variety of paper buried the harbormaster's office floor. File drawers hung open, resembling hungry mouths with empty bellies. Every cabinet had been cleaned out. The manifests and logs tossed.

It would take hours—time I didn't have—to sift through the rubble. But did I have any other choice? I had to steal a look at the harbormaster's records to confirm Sorciere's little South African excursion. I'd make up the time later. Somehow. I always did.

I scanned the wall for an emergency kit. It'd be a helluva lot easier to find the needle in this haystack with a flashlight, and I knew every emergency kit on the docks came stocked with one. It didn't take more than a minute to find the faint glow of a red medic cross. Bingo. These kits shipped with flashlights that shone brighter than the sun. At least, I thought they did. I still couldn't recall the last time I saw the big fireball in our sky.

Flashlight in hand, I tossed my raincoat on top of what looked like a chair, or it had been one in another life, and with the flashlight clenched between my lips, I fell to my knees and searched for lost treasure.

I only hoped I fared better than Lord Carnarvon and the rest of the idiots that poked their noses into Tut's tomb in Egypt and caught "the curse". Thinking on curses and plagues, I looked up and realized the green glow was gone. Upon further investigation, I found a broken window at the front end of the harbormaster's office—and it had been intact when I arrived earlier.

My instincts proved right again—someone else *had* been here, and now they were gone.

Tell Me Lies

I lost track of the hours. I tore through the thousands of scraps of paper on the harbormaster's floor but came up with nothing but lemons. Outside, the sky grew darker, gray surrendering to black. My back ached from hunching, and the gills doubled in size—and were still growing. I'd heard a ripping sound at one point, like someone tearing a piece of fabric in two, and figured the gills killed my shirt.

I made a note to visit Taylor's Threads when I could spare a minute. Besides an over-sized coat, now I needed a fresh shirt, too.

The documents containing details about *The Raven's Claw* sat buried at the bottom of the second to last pile I searched. The dates etched on their covers lined up with the dates that Sorciere broadly conveyed that morning. I tore through the loose pages. Several slipped out of the binding and floated to the floor like feathers in the wind. Official records should've held better. I checked the dates of Sorciere's pleasure cruise in the book, and I saw why the records spilled out.

Pages were missing.

Someone had torn them out in both the logbook and the manifest with precision. The missing pages matched the dates *The Raven's Claw* set out for Cape Town. Nine months ago. Someone didn't want me digging. Coincidence? There are no coincidences in this racket. Everything happens for a reason. It's all connected.

Right now, I stood on the rim of a web. I needed to find my way to the center, to the heart of the case if I wanted to solve this thing.

Time to pay the money a visit.

Your Presence Is Requested

3:35 PM

I'd get what I needed from the dame. I fished her fancy card out of my pocket and read the addresses. One for home and another for her office. Sorciere said most days I'd find her at the office.

I don't sleep on a couch, but I work late into the night. Don't you, Detective Chase?

Resolved, I headed straight to the gal's workplace. It surprised me that a dame like her worked on our side of the village. I didn't get far. A few blocks, maybe. I ran into Tommy, the paper boy. This time I did the barreling.

"We gotta stop meeting like this, Tommy."

"You ain't kidding, Mr. Down. I got so many bruises on account of bangin' into you, Miss Luna—"

Luna L'Amore. A bombshell wannabe. Peterson's personal secretary... and mistress. Who was I to judge inside my glass house?

"— is fixing to call the anonymous tip line and report my dad!"

Tommy laughed at his own joke. But I knew the Veronica Lake knock off, and she'd rat out her grandmother for pocketing cookies at the church bake sale if she'd earn a buck.

"We'll be more careful, won't we?"

I smiled at the kid. One of the few good ones left in Sweethaven. But I wondered what the kid hid under the adult-sized ball cap covering half his head.

"Yes, Mr. Down."

"Good boy."

I ruffled the kid's hair through the cap. Nothing felt out of the ordinary. I made a note to check again the next time Tommy and I ran into each other.

"See ya round the next corner, kid."

I waved and went on my way.

"Sure thing, Mr. Down!"

I listened as the kid disturbed every puddle in his path. My heart skipped a beat when the sound stopped. I turned my head just as Tommy yelled—

"Mashed potatoes and gravy! Sorry I forgot, Mr. Down."

The kid ran to me, and I spun on my heels to meet him.

"What did you forget, kid?"

"Miss Dollface asked me to give you…"

Tommy rummaged through every pocket on his person until his hands emerged, clutching a crinkled scrap of notepaper. I recognized the bargain brand. The official pad of Down Investigations.

"This!"

The kid held it up as though he'd won the Christmas raffle at Saint Francis.

"Here, I'll trade ya."

I relieved the kid of the notepaper and grabbing a small coin from my pocket, slipped it into his palm. Tommy's eyes blazed.

"Thank ya, Mr. Down! Thank ya! You're the best!"

The kid didn't stick around. He blasted off down the street, heading in the same direction as Stewart's Sweets. Tommy wasted no time spending some of his newfound wealth. A kid after my own rotten heart.

With the newsie speeding off, I unfolded the note.

Call me! ASAP! You've got company!

Company, huh? A polite way of saying "bill collector"? I didn't care for company—especially when they called without an invitation. I didn't know if Dollface sent the note as a warning or a summons. Either way, without my .38, a target hung on my gills, and hunting season was open.

Just my bad luck. I got stuck with gills instead of eyes in the back of my head. In my line of work, you couldn't put a price on an extra set of eyes. I couldn't see how I'd find a use for gills.

I'd debate the pros and cons after I collected the dough and closed the case. Rather than the longer, more direct path, I took a shortcut. It didn't shave a great deal of time off the walk, but every second matters when your back's against the wall.

The shortcut—a back alley between Ira's Instruments and the soup kitchen—proved not to be one of my better ideas. Hindsight is 20/20. I got to the halfway mark and wanted to turn around. Not just turn, but run for my life. A sort of dread crept through every crack and crevice in the alley.

I stopped long enough to find, assess, and eliminate the threat. I reminded myself to collect my .38 from Santino after I left the office. The alley held onto its secrets. Nothing stirred, but the feeling remained. A wall of mist formed at both ends of the alleyway.

"Great."

I winced as a series of sharp pains exploded through my back. Those damned gills. Growing again. Not the ideal time for a spurt. Again, why not a second pair of eyes?

The pain moved from my back to the rest of me before I could think or blink. A second later, I dropped to my hands and knees. Sweat poured off my body as I burned from the inside. Every nerve ending felt ablaze. My legs weakened and gave out on me as my back end sank to the ground. I struggled to keep my arms straight. The pain felt exquisite, doing crazy eights and wheelies under my hood.

My front end caught up to my back end, convulsing until I collapsed in a pile of sweaty flesh. I opened my mouth to scream, but I ran out of steam. I managed a wheeze and called it a day.

Then my back exploded. The pain meter dialed up to ten. I found a scream and let it rip as more of my maturing gills burst through the flesh on my back and ripped their way through my shirt, then my coat.

No way to hide them now. It was like wearing a beanie when you've got an arrow sticking out of your forehead. I lay prone, slobbering onto the pavement, praying this was it. My final curtain. I couldn't take another growth spurt. Kill me now. Don't wait until later. Show some mercy, would ya?

But the big guy checked out. No one upstairs listening anymore.

"Damn you!"

I didn't know who I meant to curse at that moment, so I considered it a blanket curse. A middle-finger to everyone.

As I prayed for a quick death, I lost sight of my surroundings. My eyes clouded over, and everything grew hazy until they'd been devoured and I saw nothing but the green-tinted fog spilling over me like wet cement.

I ran out of pleas and bargains, so I just lay there and waited for it to take me, whatever it was hiding in the mist. I heard it before I saw it. The thing's footfalls bounced off the brick walls. The pavement trembled and shook with fear. That might have been me doing the shaking.

I scanned the dark and mist as it swirled and danced around my head and face. I marveled at how graceful it moved—unlike the thing using the fog as cover. The lumbering thing coming to tear me limb from limb.

The footfalls grew louder. Closer. I knew the thing was almost on me. A massive, hulking shadow took form in the center of the fog. I'd never seen a more terrifying vision. This thing made the Mothman look like a ladybug. It stepped closer, and I almost pissed my pants.

My eyelids pulled themselves shut. Nothing to see and nothing to do now but wait to meet my maker on the other side. At least then I could say I finally made it out of Sweethaven.

"Forget this case, Dick. Take the money. Take the girl. And run. Run like the wind and don't look back. You hear me?"

I hadn't expected the thing to speak. Its voice roused me from funeral preparations. My lids peeled themselves open, and my vision adjusted. I gasped at the dark shape bending toward me. I saw it clearly then. The shape of a Herculean hulk.

A man... with an over-sized pipe tucked in the corner of his mouth.

How can I prove the guy's dead when he's looming over me larger than life? Somehow this muscled thing was Popeye the sailor guy. Now far from a pipsqueak.

"Get out. Before it's too late, Dick."

It rifled through its cavernous pockets. A second later, the thing dropped something. It hit the ground and rolled toward me, almost smacking into my head.

"This will help with your problem. But it won't cure you. Not if you stay."

A rusted can of spinach rested on its side a few inches from my head. The metal can emitted an emerald glow. I grabbed it and stuffed it into my coat pocket.

Then something changed. The air turned ice cold, and my breath came out like smoke. The hulk groaned. A mix of pain and frustration, I'd have wagered. It cried out. The shriek pierced my ears. I covered them with my hands, but it was louder in my head.

When the bellowing cry ceased, the thing snarled.

"Get out, Dick. Get out! I won't warn you again."

All at once, the thing growled and howled as it made to lunge at me. I covered my head and rolled out of its way the best I could, considering the current state of my body. Then, two powerful beams of light bore holes in the fog. Slicing through it with ease. A loud horn honked once, twice, three times before it turned into a sustained tone.

I peeked out and regarded the alley entrance with wonder. There, with headlamps blazing and fumes puffing out of a noisy exhaust, sat a car. And not just any car. One of Santino's cars.

Joey "The Wheel" Nitti poked his head through the window and waved. He honked the car's trumpet of a horn twice in short bursts that sounded like "hel-lo".

"Hey! Chase! You okay?"

Stupid question.

"I've been better."

"Don't worry! I gotchu!"

The hulking shadow slammed a fist into one of the building's walls. Bits of brick and mortar broke and dropped to the ground.

"Go," the thing said one last time.

It stood upright and thanks to The Wheel's gleaming headlights, I stole a glimpse. Before I could react, the car door opened, followed by *POP, POP, POP, POP!*

I'd recognize the sound of my .38 anywhere.

The thing huffed before it fled down the alley into the foggy dark as night closed in on Sweethaven.

Nitti hustled to me. My .38 still smoked in his hand.

"What the f... what was that thing, Chase?"

I glanced to where only a moment ago the thing towered over me.

"I don't know, Nitti. I don't know."

I lied. I knew what I saw—Popeye alive, but changed—and what I saw was impossible. Well, maybe not impossible in Sweethaven.

"That mine?" I asked as Nitti held out a hand and pulled me to my feet.

His eyes bulged.

"*Marone*, Chase! Are those... gills?"

I glanced over my shoulder at my marvelous new water breathers.

"Yeah, Nitti. I think they're gills."

The Wheel stared as if trying to compute the sight before him, and then broke into a rowdy round of laughter. He pointed at my back and laughed harder when he turned me to an angle to get a better look.

"Aw, jeez, Chase. Look at you! With the gills!"

At a loss for adequate words in this unique scene, I rolled my eyes. I grabbed my .38 and adjusted my tattered shirt and coat. My gills ached to be seen, and now they were on full display. As I turned to Nitti, I thought I saw a flicker of fluorescent green travel through my gills.

"Come on, Chase. Let's go before that thing comes back for a second round."

We walked the rest of the way in silence. Nitti only stole two looks at my fresh gills. When we reached the car, without thought or planning, we looked back at the alley at the same time. No sign of the monster.

Nitti opened a door and indicated I should get in.

"We're gonna need a bigger car I think, Chase. Those things ain't gonna fit."

"I don't know, Nitti. Whaddya say we find out?"

I ducked into the car. The tin can rattled in my pocket. I'd almost shoehorned myself into the backseat when Nitti cracked himself up.

"Wait, wait. Chase, can I touch them? Please let me touch them!"

Seeing Double

After I asked The Wheel to drop me at the office, I tuned him out. I'd grown tired of answering questions about the malignancy growing on my back. He sounded like a broken record—asking the same questions on repeat. If I didn't need The Wheel to get me to my office, I might have reached into the front seat and strangled him. I gave Nitti a day pass.

Three thoughts raced through my mind as The Wheel steered through the village. One, who. Two, do. And three, how.

Who's waiting for me at the office? Friend or foe? Maybe a snitch?

Do I tell Dollface about the humps on my back? I kept the flame of hope burning that she might not notice. Maybe the electric company would power me down for non-payment and the office would be pitch black. Dollface's plastic eyes didn't see well in the dark.

How... did Popeye the sailor guy go from meek to freak?

I know I said anything is possible in Sweethaven, but the sailor hadn't grown a simple extra toe or even gills. Popeye somehow transformed into a boogeyman. The questions I now added to the list were:

Did his lady friend know about the transformation? Did the money, Miss Sorciere? How did Popeye's metamorphosis connect to The Raven's Claw?

I checked my watch. 4:15. Dollface walked in fifteen minutes.

"Hey, Nitti?"

The Wheel eyed me in the mirror.

"Yeah, boss?"

"Be a pal and step on it? I gotta be somewhere."

"Dollface, huh? Today's the day."

Did everyone in Sweethaven know Dollface planned to split? Or had Santino guessed, and the news spread faster than pubic lice?

"Something like that."

"Better hold onto something, Chase. We're about to fly-yyyyyyyyyyy!"

The Wheel floored it. The car *BOOMED!*, then lurched forward. We blasted through Sweethaven in record-setting time. Nitti didn't know much, but in another life, he could've been a race car driver. We arrived at the office less than ninety seconds later.

"Last stop. Everybody out," The Wheel joked.

Nitti smiled and I noticed, for the first time, a shiny gold tooth in front. I did a double-take, and he must've seen me because he said, "Like it? Just got it. A gift from Santino."

A gift? From the most bloodthirsty mobster in Sweethaven? The Santino I knew didn't dole out gifts. Favors? Yes. But not gifts.

"Who'd you whack for that tooth?"

"Whack? What... what is wrong with you, Chase? I'm a driver. I drive."

"And for that, you got a fourteen-karat gold tooth?"

The Wheel snickered.

"You seen how I drive, Chase. If he gotta go like there's a fire under his ass, it's gonna come down to me and not the goons. Can't outrun a bullet."

I knew that one all too well.

"But I can outrun anything."

I tapped Nitti's shoulder and, without great ease, I slid out of the backseat. Freed from my mobile coffin, I headed for the front door. The Wheel rolled down his window and laughed.

"Hey, Chase! Come on. Let me touch them just this one time!"

He continued to plead as the door shut behind me.

"I'll show you mine if you show me yours!"

The "out of order" sign on the elevator door came as no surprise. The elevator rarely ever was in service. I took the stairs two at a time. Between the third and fourth floor, I managed a look at my watch. 4:19. The image of Dollface walking down these stairs in eleven minutes fueled my fire. I climbed the last two flights in no time and charged into my office at 4:20.

"Chase!"

I took a breath. My mouth opened and closed... *just like a fish*.

"I made it, Dollface. Ten minutes to spare."

Dollface's jaw dropped. She kept her eyes locked on me. The gills.

"Quit your gawking, Dollface. It's making me feel like a side-show freak."

She blinked for the first time in over a minute.

"It's just... Chase. Baby. You... you..."

Dollface indicated the obvious additions to my body.

"Gills. They're gills. I've seen 'em. You've seen 'em. We can talk about it later."

Her face crumbled. And so did my self-esteem. I didn't know if it was the gills or her pending exodus from Down Investigations. Or was it a tincture of both?

"I won't be here later, Chase. Today's—"

"Right. In..."

I glanced at my watch.

"Nine minutes you're leaving me and the office. You made that clear this morning, doll. But I got something that'll make you stay."

She crossed her arms on her chest and raised an eyebrow.

"Just until we close this case. I can't do it alone, Dollface. I need you."

"Chase, I—"

"Two days.

Dollface took a breath. The lines on her face faded. She closed her eyes and exhaled.

"Two days, Chase. Two."

"Thanks, Dollface. I—"

She held up a finger.

"Don't say you owe me unless you're payin'."

"Right. Hold on."

I turned to my office door.

"Where are you—"

"I told you I had something for you. Gimme a sec."

I ducked into my office, oblivious to the woman sitting in the front room. The "company". I pushed a file cabinet aside—the one packed lighter than the others, just for show—and bent to the safe hidden behind it. I flipped the dial and overheard Dollface mumble loud enough for me to "overhear".

"Two days? I gave you seven years, you big lug."

The safe door popped open. I gave the paltry contents a once-over. Nothing missing. A second .38. Four boxes of extra rounds. A list of all the safe houses in Sweethaven. And the only thing with any value—Sorciere's retainer. I peeled a bunch of bills off the pile, slid a few into my pocket, and held onto the rest. I reset the safe, tucking the cabinet back into place, and joined Dollface in the front room. The dame in the corner chair got my eye. I tipped my hat and moved to Dollface. Her arms remained tight to her chest.

"Here. It's not everything, but it's something. Go on, take it."

Dollface ogled the thin stack as though she'd never seen the green stuff. She hesitated, then grabbed the bills and stuffed them into her purse.

I moved closer to her and placed my hands on her shoulders. Her eyes looked away, but mine remained firmly in place.

"I'll give you the rest, and more, when I collect it from Sorciere. I promise. On my—"

"Do NOT say your mothah, Chase. We both know how you felt 'bout her."

I smiled. But like the clown in that opera, it masked the pain.

"Speaking of Sorciere."

Dollface tilted her head to the waiting woman. I turned to her and removed my hat. The woman rose and marched toward me and Dollface. The lack of light in that corner of the room hid the dame's face, but now that she stood in the light, I saw why Dollface sent the urgent communiqué.

"Chase, I'd like you to meet Miss—"

"Missus," the dame corrected with the sternness of a grade school-teacher.

"Sorry. MISSUS Anastacia... Sorciere."

I'd never laid eyes on this dame. The plot thickened.

The Can-Can

4:17 PM

My head whipped around to Dollface. She shrugged. I turned back to Sorciere number two and extended my hand, which she took without hesitation.

At first glance, this dame and the other could've been twins. Not carbon copies, but damned near it. The differences were slight and easy to miss if you weren't looking for them. Fewer wrinkles on this one's face. Her flawless, tight skin hugged her skull. It radiated, whereas the other's sagged and appeared dull and haggard. This dame looked ten years younger. Still, from a distance or in the right light, like a dim dick's lousy office, one could easily pass for the other.

She withdrew her hand.

"Looks like we've been two-timed, Dollface."

"I'm to take it you've met the 'other' me."

"I have, and let me say, the resemblance is..."

"Uncanny?"

"Yeah, that's a good word for it."

"You're prettier," Dollface chimed.

Sorciere number two pursed her lips.

"We're not competing in a pageant."

The air grew heavy and thick. Tense.

"Come in. Let's step into my office and talk."

I corralled the dame into my office.

"Coffee, Dollface?"

She nodded.

"Coming up."

I tapped the door shut and the dame planted her rear on the couch after inspecting it from top to bottom. Another trait shared with the other Sorciere. I eyed my chair and leaned against the edge of my desk. The added weight and size of the gills might prove too much for the rickety old thing. I spared myself the embarrassment of falling out of the chair and onto my gills.

We stared at each other until Dollface popped in with two fresh steaming mugs. I took one and she placed the other in front of the doppelgänger dame. I took a sip, desperate for the hit after my run-in with Popeye. My hands trembled. I put the mug down and hoped neither dame noticed.

I found a lone cigarette tucked into my pen holder. I held it up.

"Mind if I—"

"Yes, I do mind. I find those things abhorrent."

"Abhorrent?"

I tossed the cig into the rubbish bin. I'd feed my other addiction later.

"Yeah, Dollface. That's a fancy way of saying the Missus here doesn't approve."

Sorciere number two wrinkled her face and pursed her lips again—her go-to expression, I gathered. Sour puss. I bet this dame would never be referred to as "the life of the party".

"Why don't you start at the beginning? What do you know about this other woman?"

She slipped out of her coat. Her shape impressed, even rivaled her twin's physique. Both turned heads, but this one appeared in better shape. Fitter. Tighter. The skin on her neck looked to be wrinkle-free.

Close, but no cigar. Something else was different. Something missing on this one. I couldn't put my finger on it. I studied the dame's movements as she reached for the coffee cup, pressed it to her lips, and took a drink. She set it back on the table.

"That's actually quite good."

Dollface beamed. She opened the notepad and readied her pencil.

"Thank you, Missus Sorciere."

"When did you get wind there was another you walking around out there?"

"A few days ago. A colleague of mine rang and told me about the encounter he had with the... other woman."

"Colleague? What is it you do?"

"I don't DO any one thing, Detective Down."

"Chase. Call me Chase. Everyone else does."

"And everyone else is wrong. Etiquette says I should refer to you as 'Detective Down' and that is what I shall do."

I laughed.

"Have it your way. It's your dime."

"We'll see."

"Please, continue."

"My family owns the cannery. We have for six generations. I run it now. So that makes me the seventh."

"The cannery, huh? That's big business."

"We do... alright. We won't starve."

"Lucky you. Others in the village ain't so lucky."

The broad scowled.

"It's not for me to take care of everyone in this village. I pay a fair wage, and I expect hard work and loyalty in return."

Only guys like Santino talked about loyalty.

"My laborers receive a generous year's end bonus, paid leave, and time off for illness or family emergencies. Also paid."

"You treat them like human beings and not cattle."

"If you say so, Detective Down. If you do right by someone, they'll do right by you. That's my belief. And, so far, it's worked out."

I eyed the discarded cig.

"Paid off in green is what you mean."

"If that's how you want to put it, yes. We've done well for ourselves."

"It's the truth, ain't it? People like you think they deserve high praise and libraries dedicated to them because they do the right thing. You're no Scrooge, but I'm not patting your back."

"How disappointing." Her voice dripped with sarcasm and disdain.

"Back to the other woman. How did your 'colleague' spot the difference?"

"He didn't. At first. The woman was careful. Very careful. But she slipped."

"How so?"

"She didn't know that earlier in the day I'd decided to sell the cannery and move the business elsewhere. I already have a buyer lined up. Negotiations have been going on behind the scenes about a year now."

"A year?"

She nodded.

"Nine, maybe ten months. The deal closes in two days."

That number rang a bell.

"Things have become... troublesome in Sweethaven. I'm sure you've noticed."

I got the impression the dame meant my gills. How could I miss those?

"Sweethaven is different. Always has been."

"Look, I'll be blunt, Detective Down."

She stopped. I urged her to continue.

"By all means."

"You have gills on your back. And by next week, I suspect you'll have a lot more than that on your person. You're changing. Everyone in Sweethaven is changing. It started eight or nine months ago. Small at first. A worker here, a worker there. I brought Dr. Friedman in to examine—"

"Friedman? Why does that name ring a bell?"

"Dr. Friedman recently lost his head."

"Ah, right. 'Headless Scientist Found Dead'. But he was a scientist, right? Not the making house calls type."

"Dr. Friedman and I go way back. He was my father's personal physician before he fancied himself an explorer and scientific researcher. Amazing what a mid-life crisis and a healthy portfolio do to a man."

"So the good doctor comes in, does a check-up on some of your workers, and ends up in an alley missing his head. What was the Doc's diagnosis? Your workers. What got 'em sick?"

"Dr. Friedman didn't know. He said it was unusual. A type of toxic reaction. But he'd seen nothing like it and couldn't nail down the cause. And when it started to spread—"

"You decided to sell the joint and skip town."

"Something like that. Whatever is happening in this village, we're not the cause. I will not take the blame. The move is going to cost a substantial amount of money. I'm not happy about it, but it is necessary."

"Necessary for you, maybe. What about all the villagers you employ? They rely on the cannery to survive."

"Something is happening in Sweethaven, and I doubt in another year anyone will be left alive. If you're smart, you'll get out, too. Both of you. Get out while you can."

Popeye said the same thing.

"What is it you want me to do, Missus Sorciere?"

"I thought it would be obvious, Detective Down. Find my doppelgänger."

Let's Get Shitfaced

5:25 PM

Night came early to Sweethaven, and the first day on the case—*cases*—drew to a close. Sorciere number two left me with more questions. Two almost identical dames. How? Meanwhile, a cloud shrouded Popeye's case. I didn't have all the pieces of the puzzle, and I was no closer to figuring out what happened to the dons or who stole Tommy's papers.

I didn't like questions and no answers. Or leads. I locked up the office and grabbed a cab. The cabbie—a pockmarked guy with white hair, tattoos, and a perpetual runny nose—pretended not to notice my gills. After I gave him the address, we never spoke to one another again.

The rain returned, and I'd outgrown my raincoat. I made a second note to pay Taylor's Threads a visit first thing in the morning. I hoped Taylor had some magic left in his needles and threads. But I wondered between now and morning how much bigger my gills would grow.

Like I said—too many questions, too few answers. I instructed the cabbie to let me out on the other side of the docks. A small hole in the wall that was easy to miss. The person I needed to help me sift through the questions lived there. They liked being anonymous.

I gave the cabbie a bigger tip than he deserved, but I figured he never mentioned the gills, so in a way he'd earned it. Fifty feet separated me and the front door. I ran for it and got drenched again, anyway. I shook off the excess water and slicked back my hair. My fingers found the door buzzer, and I tapped the button twice fast, then three times slow. Our signal. An instant later, the front door lock clicked open.

I stepped into the foyer. A familiar raspy voice called down.

"Chase! I'm t'rowin' you a towel. It's raining mice and men out there. You ain't coming in 'til you get dry. Capisce? Look out."

Something fluttered above me. I saw it coming and stepped aside. An oversized bath towel hit the floor, landing with a weak thud.

"Get dry and come up. And don't forget to take off your shoes. I don't know where you dirty dicks have been."

Shitface. Informant extraordinaire. If anyone knew anything about the happenings in Sweethaven, it would be Shitface. We shared a history with some bad stretches and bad intel. But I needed the info, so I rolled the dice and tried my luck.

And yes, to satisfy your curiosity, Shitface did indeed have a pile of shit for a face. Only in Sweethaven.

The building's exterior left something to be desired, but Shitface's place looked swell. Purple velvet curtains. Matching sofa and ottoman. The thickest, softest carpet my feet ever walked on. Crystal chandeliers. China from Carson's Department Store.

I'll say it again—crime pays, no matter which side of it you're on. Unless you're a dick for hire.

I stepped in and closed the door.

"Leave the towel."

"Okay."

I dropped it by the door. The impact made a loud, squishy *SPLAT!*

I took a step and Shitface called out. "Shoes!"

I always forget the shoes. I groaned but kicked them off. House rules, and the house never loses.

Shitface lounged on a fluffy chaise under a sunlamp in the living room, working on a full-body tan. A jazz record spun on the turntable. The air smelled of incense and vanilla-scented candles. A small swarm of flies circled his head.

"A little warning next time?"

I indicated Shitface's lack of clothing.

He shrugged.

"Nothing you ain't seen before."

"Yeah. Doesn't mean I wanted to see any of it again."

"Touché, my friend. Sit. Want a drink?"

Shitface made the tastiest Manhattans. A perfect blend of bitter and sweet. But I needed to keep my wits.

"Want yes, need no. Raincheck?"

"Suit yourself, Chase. You always were a queer bird."

"You're one to talk."

"Everybody's got something in Sweethaven. Am I right? I mean, look at you now. Them gills you're trying so hard to hide on your back?"

I let my silence do the answering.

"How's it feel to be a freak, Chase? You're one of us now."

"I didn't ask for this."

"None of us did. We were chosen. Hand-picked. You should feel blessed. You're going to be part of something bigger than yourself. Bigger than all of us. Bigger than this place. You can't even imagine it. It's gonna be a beautiful dawn, Chase. A new world."

"*No comprende*, Shitface. And I think you got a—"

He swatted a fly off the tip of his nose.

"Yeah, you got it. Back it up. We were chosen by who?"

Shitface shook what little his turd head allowed.

"You got it wrong, Chase. Not who... but *what*."

Something stirred in the back of my mind. Something from a dream. My recurring nightmare of Sweethaven and the evil consuming it.

"Haven't you heard it calling you, Chase? It has. I know it has. It called out to me once, too. I followed the sound all the way to..."

Shitface smiled. He went to flash his brown teeth. A small dingleberry loosened and rolled down his chest and abdomen until it lay on the floor in a steaming pile. The flies found it with ease.

"Sorry 'bout that, Chase."

"No problem. Shit happens, right?"

"Nice to see you still got a sense of humor, Chase. You're gonna need it."

"People don't change, Shitface. You know that."

He laughed and farted at the same time. The smell hit me fast. My stomach turned over and gurgled with displeasure.

"Says the man with the gills comin' out his back. Don't fight the change, Chase."

"I need to ask you about—"

"Tell me something, Chase. You dream much?"

Coffee Break

7:19 PM

It took over an hour to steer Shitface back to answering my questions. The interrogation left me tired and cranky. I needed to think, and I needed a hit. I made my way to Flo's Coffee Shop, settled into my usual booth, and pretended not to notice the flipper that replaced Flo's left arm, and she pretended not to notice my gills.

As I sipped my joe, I reviewed my notes. I'd check on Tommy in the morning while he made his deliveries. See if any papers were missing and eyeball his body to see if it was changing. I hoped I'd find everything intact and "normal". I didn't pray, but I crossed my fingers.

My arm still hurt from the brush I had with Santino's goons.

"Flo, you got any aspirin back there?"

"Let me check, doll."

I pictured Flo trying to open the small medicine bottle with her jumbo flipper-arm. I stifled a laugh when she threw me the bottle from behind the counter—with her good arm.

"Help yourself, Chase."

And I did. I dry swallowed three and pocketed four more. Just in case. I thought about tossing her the bottle, but left it on the counter on the way out.

Nitti said Santino feared for his life. Wanted a quick getaway if it came to that. Santino seemed cool as a cucumber when I spoke to him.

Curious, maybe. Scared? No. Santino stood to gain plenty with the competition on ice. But then why drag me into it? Was hiring me a cover story? Something to keep me distracted while he made another play.

I left Shitface with only one valuable scrap of intel—don't trust Santino.

He'd also told me to listen for its call, so maybe Shitface needed an enema to clear his head.

I tore a few pages out of my notepad and put them in a line. On each, I wrote something different—

Tommy/Missing papers

Santino/Missing dons

Popeye/Missing? Dead? Neither?

The Raven's Claw/What happened nine months ago?

The two Sorcieres/Unknown variable

Not much to go on. Tomorrow, I'd take a trip to two addresses the fake Sorciere engraved on her fancy card. Then I'd work my way through the names of the crew who sailed with Popeye on *The Raven's Claw*. And if I was still standing and not swimming with the fishes, I'd pay a visit to Giuseppe's Ristorante on Mott. A known mobster hangout. Somebody might part with a bit of information for the right price. I had little to spend, but if it helped put the pieces together, so be it.

"Good night, Flo. See ya in the morning."

I tapped the aspirin bottle on the counter along with enough change to cover my bill with something extra for Flo. I got as far as the door when I stopped to wonder if Flo ever went home. Or did she have a couch in the back she slept on like me?

I pushed at the door, readying to brave the rain. A bell clanged above it. It made a pitiful sound. For a spell, I watched the rain illuminated by the flickering streetlamps. The surface shimmered. The rainwater ran like a stream into the sewer grates on both sides at the end of the streets. A heavy mist leaked out of the sewer. The water appeared green in its emerald glow.

The rain pelted my face as I stepped outside. Something rattled behind me, and I turned to see Flo holding up her flipper arms. Both now changed. She smiled and waved a flipper in my direction.

"Do you dream much, Chase?"

Dead Ends Meet

7:57 PM

I felt wired. Jazzed up on caffeine and aspirin. Every dick's favorite double-header. I rummaged through my pockets and remembered the can of spinach. Talk about queer. I left the spinach and took the list of sailors the fake Sorciere handed over this morning. Jeez, was that only this morning?

The night was young enough to cross a few names off the list, and maybe swing by Sorciere's place of employ, and the residence at the top of Rattle Snake Hill. Nighttime is the best time to stage a confrontation. Why? Easier to get lost in the dark if it goes sideways, which it always does. I tapped my .38 and headed to the first address on the list.

The rain made the short walk feel long. When I arrived at the address, I found a vacant lot with a lopsided "For sale" sign stuck in the middle of an overgrown lawn. Can't say I was surprised. I crossed Mackenzie Addams off my list.

I headed to the second address, which turned out to be "Half Mast", a pub frequented by seafarers. Put a buck on the bar and broke sailors lined up to spill their beans. I left the bar twenty minutes later, three bucks lighter, but with the info I needed.

Sailor number two, Kevin Kilroy, died six months ago—three months after returning from the imposter's voyage to Cape Town.

My streak of bad luck continued as I crossed the third name off the list. The guy disappeared six weeks ago. No one had heard a peep since. Could have skipped out over a debt, but it didn't feel right. My gut said sailor number three, Leo Lipschitz, was still out there somewhere.

One name left on the list. Artie Asher. I knew of Artie but never met the guy face to face. We had a mutual friend who'd let drop that Artie was the always looking for work type—which translated to Artie didn't mind getting his hands dirty for a buck. Smart and even-tempered. The guy you wanted at your back.

I charmed Artie's landlady, Helga Gildernstine, into loaning me the keys to Artie's pad. She blushed when I asked her where I could find Artie. The dame didn't need a dime to talk. And once she started, she had no "off" switch.

Helga's story was that Artie went off the deep end about eight months ago—one month after the South African voyage. I pushed for specifics, and she told me that Artie was convinced there was a cult in Sweethaven. We both laughed at the absurdity of the accusation, but I wondered if it really was a stretch. There were gills on my back. How unbelievable was a cult?

Artie's current address was Arkham Asylum. Not a tourist destination. His studio apartment was paid up for a year, which Helga thought odd since Artie paid the rent a day or two or eleven late.

So who flipped his bill? And why?

I asked Helga why she kept him on, and she said, "Late or not, a good tenant is a good tenant. Artie? Never made a fuss. Respectful. Good morning, ma'am. Hello, ma'am. His mother did him right. He didn't make much noise. Until..."

"Until eight months ago."

She nodded as though giving the executioner the signal to bring down the axe.

I let myself in and shut the door on the old gal. Her lips still flapped for another five minutes before she took her leave.

Artie's place appeared small by most standards, but he made good use of it. Organized. Strange considering Helga said Artie "went off the deep end". I rifled through the sailor's stuff, careful not to disturb anything. I intimated Artie was the guy who knew when a hair fell out of place.

Nothing unusual jumped out. A few books, *Moby Dick* among them, an open tab at Half Mast, and a laundry ticket. I rummaged through his coat and pants pockets and found a ball of lint, a stiff stick of bubble gum, a broken cigarette—a waste, if you ask me—and some pocket change totaling sixty-two cents.

Convinced I'd hit another dead end, I headed for the door. My finger landed on the light switch, but instead of clicking it, I turned and took a last look at Artie's place. And that's when I noticed it. Something taped under the desk. I didn't see it before because I'd been standing in the wrong place. Now, in the right spot in the room and with my investigative eyes on the case, it screamed at me.

I peeled back the tape, and a small book fell into my hands, and something slid out from the pages and landed a few feet away. The faded letters spelled out "Journal". I thumbed through the pages and, as advertised, the book contained Artie's accounts of his days, deep thoughts, and peculiar drawings.

One thing that struck me right away—Artie's handwriting in the later pages appeared frantic. Disjointed. Fragments of thoughts. Maybe he'd gone off the deep end after all?

I flipped the pages back. I wanted to see what Artie jotted down while on the doppelgänger's vacation vessel. Jackpot. He'd written plenty. Too much. I needed to take this back to the office and study it page by page, word by word. This was my first real clue, ignoring the monstrous Popeye.

I tucked the notebook in my back pocket and went for the small white paper that slipped out of the book. I turned it over. It was a photo, and not just any photo. This was taken on the deck of *The Raven's Claw*—the ship's name clearly visible in the bottom corner of the photo. The ship impressed. It looked European in design. Sleek and elegant. Not boxy or bulky. *The Raven's Claw* was made to do one thing—slice through the sea at high speed.

On the deck stood five sailors dressed from head to shoe in white, and six middle-aged guys that looked like they stepped out of a college lecture hall. A trendily dressed man in glasses hid behind the row of sailors and professors. I got the sense he didn't want to be in the photo but was coerced into it. Maybe in the spirit of comradery or celebrating the launch? But who was this guy and what was his contribution?

Missing was the money. "Sorciere".

I tucked the photo into Artie's journal when I had a flash. Sorciere's eye-catching necklace. I grabbed the photo and brought it as close to my face as I could before it grew too blurry to see. Without a magnifier I couldn't be positive, but with my naked eye I'd swear the stiff in the back row had something dangling on his neck. Was it a necklace? I couldn't be sure until I got a closer look. It could've been a cigarette burn on the film. I made a note to get a closer look at it later.

Snake Eyes

10:36 PM

Before heading back to the office, I checked out the dame's addresses. I started with the office address since she'd said she practically lived there, and it was a five-minute walk from Artie's place. Maybe six minutes in the rain.

A building once stood at 6527 Spade Way, but not anymore. A charred steel skeleton rose out of the ashes. Whatever took it down happened months ago. The dame lied. Again.

I took a taxi to Rattle Snake Hill. Although I found a large house looming in the fog, neither of the silver-haired homeowners fit the "Sorciere" bill. Another dead end.

The dame came to me prepared with a story, a bag of dough, and a pre-printed calling card. It'd been planned. Now I just needed to find out *why*.

The Midnight Hour

By the time I made it back to the office, I was dead on my feet. Flo's cup o' joe ran out of kick, and the rain punishing my body outstayed its welcome. But it always rains in Sweethaven now.

The office came into view, and I quickened my step, anxious to end this endless day. I stepped off the curb into the street and out of nowhere, a figure banged into me. He jumped at me like a rabbit from a magician's hat. I braced for the fall. Still, the ground hurt like a mother—

"Hey, pal! Watch it!"

The shape, which was wearing a burlap cloak, turned.

"Open your—"

I stopped as his face came into view. Pale. Thin. Marked with several boils that looked ready to expel their load. And in place of his eyes, two green orbs glowed.

I recoiled when he extended a hand, but soon took it. He pulled me up with enormous strength and ease. As my head met the bottom of his pointy chin, the brand on his chest caught my attention—a circle made of tentacles with a giant pair of octopus-like eyes in the center. The same design as "Sorciere's" family heirloom.

"Uh, thanks. Say, pal. That's a curious mark you got there. Where'd you get it? I'd like one for myself. I love octopuses. Octopi?"

The cloaked man smiled. Something told me to run, but I stayed put.

"He sees you. Answer the call. Follow the music. The Awakening is almost at hand. Prepare, brother."

He released my hand and strode into the rain.

"How long? How long until this Awakening? Come on! Give me something!"

I'd given up hope the mystery monk would utter another word. But just as he faded into the mist, he called back, "Two days..."

I checked my watch. 12:01. Two days remained on "Sorciere's" clock. I just needed to find the dame first.

The Great Escape

12:10 AM – Day 2

I didn't know what it all added up to, but my gut did somersaults and cartwheels the more I turned the cases over in my mind. I wondered if Popeye'd been right. Should I drop the cases? Pretend none of this day happened?

Then I thought about Tommy, and the gills growing on my back, and I couldn't walk away. Not yet. I felt the answers coming closer and getting clearer. Two days to piece it all together. And when the timer expired? I didn't know.

If the forecast called for trouble, the killing kind, I wanted Dollface away from it. Everyone seemed to know about our relationship, and that made her an easy tool to get to me. For both our sakes, Dollface needed to vamoose until the dust settled. I'd been wrong to mix her up in it. I should've just let her go.

She'd been sleeping when I called and told her to get out of town. The conversation lasted about three minutes. I didn't know if I'd convinced her, but I hoped she possessed the good sense to get the hell out of Sweethaven.

I retired to the couch. The pain in my back resumed its torture. The gills were about to grow again. I remembered the can of spinach and what Popeye said in the alley—*this will help with your problem.*

I felt like gambling, so I pried open the can. It stank like a swamp. Worse. I heaved, but the pain in my back won out. I slurped several mouthfuls of the toxic green until I couldn't stand to eat anymore. Kept it down, no small feat. I fell back onto the couch and waited. Sure enough, ten minutes later, the gills stopped tearing up my back.

I fell into a peaceful sleep, but it didn't last long. The phone rang and rang. The clock on the wall read 1:47 AM. I sleepwalked to my desk and picked up the receiver.

"Yeah?"

"Chase! Oh my god, Chase!"

Dollface.

I woke up fast.

"What is it? What's wrong?"

She started crying on the other end. The line popped and hissed with static. Outside, the rain fell heavier than ever.

"The fog, Chase. The fog!"

"Yeah, what about it, Dollface?"

"It's surrounded the village."

Dollface shrieked and sobbed. I moved the receiver away from my ear. I checked my ear to see if it was bleeding.

"Whaddya mean 'surrounded'? Make sense, Dollface."

"It's like a wall, Chase. We're trapped inside. There's no way out."

And that's when I realized whoever moved the pawns into position just called "check". Less than forty-eight hours remained to block a "checkmate".

Shadows Fall

3:14 AM – Day 2

Dollface snored on the office couch. Given the latest development, I wanted eyes on her. I needed to think, and I couldn't sift through the clues and worry about Dollface at the same time. My wits needed to be sharp. Focused. And I knew how to jolt my brain cells awake.

I clicked the light switch on my way out. Darkness swallowed my office in one gulp. Dollface's sleeping form blended with the couch, camouflaged. If you didn't know she was there, it'd be easy to miss her. I left my spare .38 on the table just in case anyone came calling while I was out. Dollface wasn't a crackerjack shot, but good enough to send a boy scout packing.

I slurped a mouthful of spinach and headed out into the relentless rain. I didn't bother to put on a shirt or slip into my raincoat. The gills hadn't gotten any bigger in the last few hours, but they were still big enough that nothing fit over them. I figured the residents had enough to worry about to notice the cross I bore on my back.

On the walk to Flo's coffee shop, I noticed half a dozen of those monks in the burlap robes. They ignored me, and I ignored them. Other than the green glow of the brand on their chests, they looked identical to the one I'd encountered last night. They mumbled words that might've been a foreign language. I was no linguist, but it had the flavor of Latin. Yet it sounded older like Latin evolved from it. I caught an occasional "…itch" but I couldn't make out the word that preceded it. For all I knew, the monks could've been walking the streets of Sweethaven in search of a sand-wich.

Flo's place looked locked up. A lone light shone over the counter. The proprietor was nowhere in sight. I gave the door handle a tug and, to my surprise, the door popped open. The bell sounded. It rang louder than usual in the eerie silence. The door swung shut as I headed for the counter.

"Flo? You back there?"

The quiet offered no reply.

"Flo? Everything okay?"

I stood at the counter, eyeing the pass-through. I couldn't make out a thing. Total darkness. I tapped the "ring for service" bell on the counter several times and waited. Other than the rain on the window, the shop was dead quiet. I slapped at the bell a dozen times until something stirred in the kitchen. I eased up on the bell, tapping my .38 with a shaky hand. Better safe than sorry.

"Who goes there?"

It sounded like Flo, but different. Sleepy, as though her head was still in a dream.

"Chase."

"Oh."

Rustling in the kitchen. A clang and clatter. Sounded like a pot or a pan hitting the floor. A loud *THUD!* followed. Heavy, uneven footsteps.

"Hey, you okay, Flo?"

The dame laughed. The hairs on my neck rose to attention. My fingers wrapped around the handle of my .38 as the lumbering footsteps moved closer to the swinging doors.

"Neverrr… betterrrrr, d-d-dear."

She didn't sound better. Flo sounded... changed. My mouth went dry, and a cold bead of sweat dribbled down my forehead. The door creaked open, and Flo ambled into the light. I swallowed a gasp. I should've been used to it by now, but every now and then, Sweethaven throws me for a loop.

In a matter of a few hours, the waitress I'd known for years, who served me coffee and toast every morning, and always had my booth and a cup o' joe waiting for me, transformed into a human-sized fangtooth fish. She managed a grin, and those long, protruding fangs chomped at the air. A tiny phosphorescent gray dot in the center of her circular black eyes glimmered.

I eased my grip on the .38 and got to the point. I'd rather walk in the pouring rain than watch the thick rope of clear goo ooze out of Flo's mouth. She suggested I brew my own pot of coffee on account of her condition. I jumped behind the counter and helped myself, avoiding eye contact with the ferocious-looking fish. The sweet aroma of my elixir stirred my senses.

"Hey, Flo. Do you know of anything happening in Sweethaven tomorrow?"

If anyone knew of a happening, it'd be Flo. She was keyed into everything in Sweethaven.

Flo mashed her fangs. Her dark, unblinking eyes stared at me as though she wanted to take a hearty bite out of me.

"Happening, d-d-dear?"

"Yeah, like, I don't know... a parade or festival in the square?"

She opened her mouth, revealing a large dark tunnel that led to certain death. It snapped shut like a bear trap as her fangs sparkled in the light.

"Hmm. Nothing comes to mind. But..."

The coffee was done. I filled as many Styrofoam to-go cups as I could carry, which turned out to be two. The cups burned my hands as though they were hot coals.

"But?"

"Tomorrow is a full moon."

A shadow passed over Flo's fishy face. She uttered a low chant in the same strange language the monks outside mumbled. Again, the only sound I recognized was "...itch". I teetered on my feet. The coffee shop spun like a carnival ride. The green glow running through my gills brightened and dimmed like a homing beacon.

Flo continued chanting as I struggled to keep my balance. The cups slipped from my hands. The hot coffee burned through my shoes, rousing me from whatever waking nightmare overtook me. I jumped over the counter and dashed to the door. The bell clanged as I opened it and stepped into the rain. The cold water soothed the burning in my feet.

As the door swung shut, Flo called out, "Be a d-d-dear and lock up, won't you?"

I didn't look back, and I didn't lock the door. I steered myself through the village like Nitti behind the wheel. Shadows fell in all directions. Endless night. The once peaceful seaside village of Sweethaven succumbed to the evil infection as it sank into shadow.

All the News Fit to Print

5:27 AM – Day 2

I wandered the unfamiliar streets. I felt like I'd stepped into one of those psychedelic abstract paintings I saw in a gallery once. Dollface's idea, not mine. I went along to smooth things over after the wax museum failed to dazzle.

In less than twenty-four hours, the once peaceful seaside village of Sweethaven turned into a wasteland as the pestilence spread. The village showed symptoms of its sickness. The sewers overflowed with a green slime. Rats scurried into the darkest corners, their green eyes staring out of the pitch black. Two dozen or more mumbling monks stumbled through the rain, chanting and whispering in that strange foreign tongue.

I wondered what the place would be like tomorrow. If it'd even still be a small dot on the map, or if outsiders would tell our story alongside the lost colony of Roanoke. The stuff of legend and ghost story. Less than forty-eight hours remained on the clock to find the cure.

I encountered Tommy near the docks. The kid appeared in a hurry, so I kept the interrogation—and physical inspection—brief. A tap on the ball cap revealed no malignancies. A silver lining.

"Jeez, Mr. Down! Are those... gills?"

I sighed and nodded.

"Yes, Tommy. I have gills now."

He ran his fingers down the length and giggled. Nitti would be cross with Tommy if he saw the newsie putting hands on my aqua lungs.

"Neat-o! I think they're cool."

"Glad you think so, kid. I'm still getting used to them myself. Say, where's the fire?"

Tommy rolled his eyes.

"Short stack?"

"Nah, even worse, Mr. Down. No stack! No papers. Can you believe it?"

My stomach sank.

"Has that ever happened before, Tommy?"

His forehead wrinkled, and he squinted an eye.

"I don't think so. Is that bad, Mr. Down?"

"I think it is, kid."

Tommy leaned in.

"It's like what's happening in the village, ain't it?"

Smart kid. Connected the dots on his own.

"Maybe. Where were you headed just now?"

The kid groaned and threw back his head. The ball cap slipped but did not fall off. His hands rushed to adjust it. I wondered if the kid was hiding something under it after all.

"Mr. Peterson. Emergency meeting."

"At the printing press?"

Tommy tilted his head.

"No, he gave us an address. Here."

He dug into his pocket and retrieved a slip of paper with what looked like a hastily written address. I knew the place. A warehouse between the backside of the cannery and the south end of the docks. It didn't feel right. I fished a couple of bills out of my wallet.

"Hey, kid. Do me a favor?"

Tommy eyed the bills for a second, then snatched them up.

"Sure, Mr. Down. Name it! Anything for you. You're all right. Not a creep or anything."

I made a note to ask the kid when this was over, who'd been the creep. I planned on making a house call.

"Don't go to the meeting."

"But Mr. Peterson will fire me. We need the money, Mr. Down. My dad—"

"Leave that to me. I'll have a word with your boss."

A word or a fist. Same difference to me. I'd wanted to slug Peterson's smug face since the seventh grade. I grabbed my pad and pencil and jotted down a name and an address. I ripped out the page and handed it to the kid. Might as well kill two birds with one stone. The kid was already an honorary 'Irregular'—as in Sherlock's Baker Street Irregulars.

"Hong and Dong and Company?"

Tommy laughed at the word "dong" as boys his age do.

"Yes. I need you to tell me everything you can about the place. A Mr. Moser in particular. Ronald J. Moser. Meet me back at the office."

The kid stuffed the paper into his shirt pocket along with the dough. He took off toward Hong and Dong and Co., which sat far enough away from where Peterson called a meeting of Sweethaven's paperboys. I figured I'd let Tommy scope out Moser while I got a look at what my old chum Peterson got himself into.

"Sure thing, Mr. Down! See ya!"

I waved, but the kid was as good as dust in the wind with his back to me. And yet, he waved back. Queer. I made a note and headed to the warehouse. I hoped I'd done the right thing sending Tommy on a side mission.

One way to find out.

Laughing Gas

I drew my .38 as soon as the warehouse came into view. A heavy mist crept out from under the door and through every splintered window frame and crack in the bricks. Inside, an emerald glow flared. Its light should have been blinding, but my eyes looked on it without discomfort.

The closer I got to the place, the rottener the smell. It reminded me of the noxious noseful I'd inhaled at the harbormaster's office, only more pungent. I masked my nose with my free hand and quickened my pace. A low hum emanated from inside the warehouse. The more I listened, the more I realized it wasn't a hum but the low, murmuring chant I'd heard all morning.

"...itch."

My heartbeat sounded like an atomic bomb in my ear. I went for the door. Pad locked, bolted from the inside, and a heavy piece of lumber nailed across the doors for extra measure. I tugged at the door anyway, knowing it wouldn't budge, and gagged as the smell enveloped me in a toxic cloud. I pinched my nose closed and ran to a side window. Someone had soaped it. The other windows sported a similar look.

Through the blur, I discerned a dozen or more paper boys gathered around a pulsating green object. I smashed the window with the butt of my .38. A rush of fumes blew past my face. I held my breath. My eyes watered and my cheeks burned. And once the warehouse expelled enough gas, the horrible picture came into view.

Every newspaper boy in Sweethaven lay dead. Their open mouths bubbled with a sudsy white foam. A thin stream of blood dripped from their noses. Someone gassed the boys. I'd observed similar deaths during the war. Horrible ending to short lives.

I didn't see Tommy among the dead. A tiny victory in a major defeat.

Pete Peterson Dodges a Bullet

After I'd punished myself enough for not getting to the warehouse sooner, I headed for the main building of the *Sweethaven Sun*. I figured I'd smoke that rat Pete Peterson from his nest. Someone needed to answer for those boys. Take responsibility and take the punishment I doled out. Peterson's face had it coming.

I took the stairs. No use in announcing my presence. But I found the place deserted, and the equipment turned off. There'd be no *Sweethaven Sun* printed today. A small grace. The overhead lights felt cold, as though they'd been dark at least a few hours. Maybe more. I wondered if Peterson didn't gas his personnel in another warehouse across town.

I found his office on the top floor. The desk lamp was switched on. Its soft yellow light cast long, ominous shadows on the walls. Static hissed over a radio. I turned the volume down. My ears needed to focus.

Peterson sat at his desk in a perfectly serviceable chair. I envied the guy his chair. He'd turned to peer out the floor-to-ceiling window behind the desk, though the view left a lot to be desired even on a good day. If Peterson heard me come in, he ignored my presence.

"Peterson? Hey, Pete!"

I grabbed the .38 and readied to fire.

"Pete? I'm coming over. Don't make any—"

Pete's chair swirled around. At once I saw the guy was dead. Something got to one side of his round face. Gnawed it down to the bone. An enormous hole stood in place of a nose. Blood drenched the front of his open shirt. And there, dead center, the brand. Tentacles circling octopus eyes. Blood traveled through the curves as though it were a mouse in a tunnel.

I lowered the .38 and stepped back.

"Jeez, Pete. What the hell happened to you? You had to go and get your face chewed on before I could tenderize it. Typical."

I went for the lamp, moving to shine it on Pete's mangled face to get a better look, when his mouth fell open. His tongue wiggled out of his open mouth and rolled down the length of his body until it splattered on the floor.

I raised the .38.

Something squeaked and slithered inside Pete's throat. Blood leaked out from the corners of his mouth. The sound of the squeaking and slithering grew louder. Now the blood gushed out Peterson's mouth like a chocolate fountain.

Gurgle. Gurgle. Squeakkkk. Slitherrrrr.

My heart stopped as two small green eyes stared out at me from the back of Peterson's throat. It inched closer to the exit and chittered in a pitch close to Miss Oyl's tedious voice. The creature wormed forward. A grayish-green tentacle whipped out of the muckraker's mouth, followed by seven more. It poked its head under Peterson's top teeth and then raised itself upright, whirling its eight tendrils.

The octopus's eyes locked on me. Their glow intensified. It chittered and shrieked as it lowered its bulbous head and shrank onto its tentacles. Then the creature fell silent. If it weren't for the glowing eyes, I might've thought the thing expired after feasting on Pete Peterson.

But it lived and, in an instant, flung itself off Pete's mouth as though it was a diving board, hurling itself into the air, across the desk—headed straight at ME!

I fired three slugs into the blob. It howled with every hit, flailing its tentacles in all directions. A thick green substance I took for its blood covered the back window. The octopus gave one final twitch, and then it dropped to the floor. I kicked at it to confirm it was dead. A bit of goo got on my shoe, but the creature remained still.

I slowed my breath and tucked away the .38. The room looked fuzzy, so I steadied myself on a corner of Peterson's executive desk. I panted and fought for air. My chest tightened and something burned under my hood.

As I reached into my pocket to take a hit of the spinach, I found a note on Peterson's desk. The handwriting resembled his, from what I remembered. And the note'd been penned on personalized stationery.

"I had no choice. I'm sorry, boys…"

Peterson got lucky. Something else did him in before my fists had their fun with his smug mug. Being hollowed out by an otherworldly octopus was the easier way to go.

Do Not Pass Go

I descended the stairs with the octopus's corpse wrapped in Peterson's rag of a paper. I'd finally found a use for the rag. The dead thing's sour smell burned through the paper. I gripped the banister as I focused on each step. My vision remained unfocused, and my head felt heavier than a hearty slice of Flo's New York cheesecake.

I rested at the halfway mark. The spinach soothed the savage gills, but the residual pain knocked the wind out of me. My eyes closed, and behind them I felt a massive shadow cover the stairwell. I didn't need to open my eyes to know the shadow was Popeye.

"I told you to leave it alone. Get out."

The sailor's rough voice sounded like gravel.

"Yeah, well, no one can get out now, huh, Popeye? Fogged in. Trapped like drowning rats in all this rain. You know it never stops raining in Sweethaven? You notice that?"

Popeye laughed.

"Do you *dream* much, Chase?"

My heart skipped a beat.

"Why... do you ask?"

"Don't answer its call."

"I'll let it ring. Dollface'll take a message."

"Find a place to lie low. Underground. The deeper the better. Bring the girls."

"Girls?"

"Dollface and Olive."

"Right. When are we going underground?"

"Before the full moon. You can come out the morning after, when I've taken care of it."

"How will I know if—"

"You'll know. If I fail, there won't be a morning."

"Wait a minute, bub. What do you mean... take care of 'it'?"

"The reason for all of this. The changes. Nights that don't end. Haunting dreams. And the call."

"Yeah, but who's doing the calling?

"The Eldritch. The Old One."

The penny dropped.

The chant. *Eldr-itch*.

"An ancient god."

Like Pieces of a Puzzle

6:39 AM – Day 2

The one-eyed sailor kept it brief, which I appreciated. The only useful exchange went like this—

"That you bustin' heads, or should I say poppin', all over town?"

"No, it's... another."

I blew a raspberry.

"Them eyewitnesses got it wrong? Every one of them? You're not the 'hulking shadow' going round the village decapitating and muti-lating scientists?"

The shadow moved. Popeye shaking his giant head.

"It. Wasn't. ME."

"Right, bub. You expect me to believe there's another hulking sailor—"

Another. *Two.* Similar but not exact. Opposite sides of the same coin.

Two.

Sorciere.

Two versions of the dame walked the streets of Sweethaven.

A piece of the puzzle slid into place.

Plastic People

7:19 AM – DAY 2

I returned to the office. Dollface put the coffee on. The musty place smelled of the sweet brown beans. I threw myself onto the couch and reviewed what I had so far in my notes.

"You hear from Tommy, Dollface?"

"Was I supposed to?"

"Yeah."

"Then, no."

Be okay, kid. Be okay.

Somewhere out in the fog, there were two Sorcieres and two Popeyes. Neither individual had twins, so how could this be? Someone wanted to silence the news. Control it. To get it, they murdered Pete Peterson and his newsies. Peterson had the strange brand on his chest. Burlap-sack-clad monks. Mumbling some kind of... incantation? All wear the brand. Imposter Popeye was killing every scientist he sailed with on a voyage commissioned by the fake Sorciere. Real Sorciere owns the cannery. Moving out.

No sign of the missing dons. Santino criticized Peterson's rag. He told me about the missing dons, but it doesn't clear him in their disappearances. Santino could have dispensed with them discreetly and kept it out of the news. The cannery is moving, and territory is ripe for the picking. The one who controls the land and sea in Sweethaven is king. And Santino wasn't shy about admitting he wanted it all.

The top part fit, but not the bottom. How was Santino involved with Popeye's ill-fated voyage? Why kill a bunch of scientists you never met? Or did Santino know them? Was he the real money behind *The Raven's Claw*? Was the imposter Sorciere a distraction? A face to the shadow running things in the dark... Santino? But then who was the face that hid in the back row in the photo I found at Artie's place? Who was HE, and how did he fit in with Santino and Sorciere?

A fake nose here and a lift there can make any dame look like a movie star. I've seen enough fake Lana Turners and Gloria Grahames to last two lifetimes. But did Santino have the means to fake a monstrous Popeye? He had the dough. And he had the motive, but did Don Santino have... *the scientists?*

The Great Flood

8:15 AM – DAY 2

I sent Dollface packing. I told her to keep it light. It was an all-ex-pense-paid, two-night stay, not a honeymoon in Fiji. I got one of her patented looks, but she promised to try. I couldn't ask for more than that.

I hit the streets to look for Tommy. I saw the kid three hours ago. He should've checked in by now. My stomach bubbled with acid. I needed the kid to be okay. If he walked into a landmine, that was on me. I gave the marching orders.

I rounded back to where we'd started—on the docks, near the warehouse where the boys had been gassed. No sign of Tommy. No ball cap. No blood. Nothing. I took it as a hopeful sign. I found the address for Hong and Dong and charted a course.

Not even nine in the morning, and the sky was pitch black. No stars. I wondered how the moon would find a place to shine. The rain flooded the streets. I altered course several times to avoid the rising waters. If the rain didn't let up, Sweethaven would be underwater before tomorrow night's moon rising. Hell, Sweethaven might be underwater before lunchtime today.

I got turned around on the backstreets. I never frequented this corridor of the village, so the streets were unfamiliar to me once the flooding forced me off the main thoroughfare. Kicking at a puddle of rain, I threw my arms up in surrender. I never imagined I'd need a map to find my way in a village the size of Sweethaven.

I retraced my steps to the warehouse. From there, I'd wade through the water on the familiar path if I had to. Two blocks retraced and the road vanished. Taken by the rising waters.

As the water rose, it took on a bright green glow. The mist and fog rolled in off the sea. The streets that weren't flooded were lost in the thick haze. I picked a direction and kept moving. The longer I stood still, the harder it'd be to find my way back to the docks.

The water felt heavy like sand. It slowed my progress. I rounded a familiar-looking bend and took another turn I thought I recognized. A couple more turns, and the main street came into view through the mist. I dragged my feet through the water and realized despite the physical exertion, my breath came easily. No panting or wheezing. Most days, five flights of stairs were enough to do me in. And trudging through those flooded streets had felt like climbing up and down the Eiffel Tower in a fitted pair of cement shoes.

I neared the familiar streets, and the next thing I knew, something tackled me and dragged me under the water. I fought to breathe, swallowing toxic rainwater as my mouth opened and closed. On the verge of drowning, the one doing the drowning lifted me out of the water.

"Don't say a word, Detective Chase. Don't even breathe."

The grip around my neck loosened. I expelled a gallon of water.

"Who are you? What do you want?"

"I'm Leo Lipschitz."

Lipschitz alive.

"As for what I want... that's more complicated."

Leo Loses His Head

"Mind letting go of my neck, Lipschitz? I'd like to breathe in some of Sweethaven's good, old poisonous fumes."

Leo hesitated, but eased until my neck gained its freedom. I stumbled forward, putting Leo at an arm's length as I sucked in air. I kept the guy close enough to shoot if he got any crazy ideas but far enough away so I could breathe easy.

"Sorry, Detective Chase. I'm on edge, you see."

I turned to Lipschitz. The guy cowered, but I glimpsed the dark circles under his eyes, the unkempt hair protruding from the hood of his rain slicker and a beard that hung down to the middle of his chest. And something glowed green under that hood. I suspected Leo didn't want me to see the cause.

"Have you been to Artie's place?"

I nodded, coughing up green water.

"Nothing extraordinary."

"Did you recover Artie's journal, Detective Chase?"

I gave Lipschitz a sideways glance.

"Oh, I know all about the journal. I told him to keep it... just in case."

"In case of what?"

Leo turned his head to the sky and raised his arms to say *all this.*

"We did this, Detective Chase. We're responsible."

I stood upright. A rage ignited in my belly. People died. Peterson. The newsies. Some others went missing. And the rest of us were changing. Tommy...

"What did you do, Lipschitz? What did you guys do in South Africa?"

Leo laughed.

"South Africa? No, Detective Chase. We sailed all the way north. The Arctic Circle. So many wonderful secrets buried under thousands of years of ice. You can't fathom what we found up north."

"Let me take a guess: an ancient god from another dimension?"

"Oh, maybe you can. Did you see the photo?"

I shrugged.

"In Artie's journal. The photo of the crew on the deck?"

"Yeah, I stumbled on it. What about it?"

"It was taken just prior to setting sail. If I'd known what horrors awaited us... what it was we brought back... I would have jumped ship."

"Like Popeye?"

Lipschitz gasped and retreated a foot or two.

"You know about Popeye?"

"I know he sailed off with you guys, and then didn't make it back. Heard he fell off the ship, then either drowned or got served up raw to the sharks."

Leo laughed. I recoiled at the sound.

"Popeye didn't fall or jump. He was pushed."

"Let me get this straight, Lipschitz. You're saying Popeye—"

"—was murdered? Yes."

Leo muttered something I didn't catch, but I heard enough to know it wasn't the same cosmic tune that'd become so popular with everyone else in Sweethaven.

"I have to go. I can't stay here."

Lipschitz backed up and fell into the water. He retreated on his hands and knees. Water slapped his face.

"There's no way out, Leo. We're locked inside the snow globe that is Sweethaven."

He got to his feet.

"Can't stay here. Cannot linger anywhere. Have to keep moving or he'll find me."

"Come with me, Leo. I can help. We'll end this together."

"Talk to Artie in Arkham. And look at the picture again. Look... closely, Detective Chase. When you see it, you'll understand what you're asking me to face. My sin is unforgivable, but I'll settle that at the gates with St. Peter."

Lipschitz turned to run, or trudge, as fast as his legs could push through the flood water.

"Have to keep moving. Can't stay in one—"

Lipschitz never uttered another word.

A second later, a massive shadow rose out of the water. Lipschitz screamed as a swirling fog surrounded him and the shadow. Without hesitation, the hulk ripped Leo's head off his neck. The torso fell forward and bobbed in the red water. A second later, something crashed, and the water splashed in front of me. I looked down and saw Lipschitz's face, frozen in terror, staring up at me.

The shadow hulk stepped through the fog and if it wasn't the spitting image of Popeye the sailor guy, it was a near perfect copy—this one the dark foil to the other.

I got the sense the creature wasn't there for me. Lipschitz was the mark. I dove into the glowing water and swam for my life. Blocks and blocks later, when my arms grew tired, I stole a look over my shoulder.

The thing was nowhere in sight.

A Not So Long Kiss Goodbye

10:41 AM – DAY 2

I returned to the office. I prayed, I did, that Tommy'd be kicking back reading a comic book on the couch. No Tommy, but Dollface had packed the right bag for the nights ahead. Now I just needed to stash her somewhere until after the full moon.

I perused the list of safe houses I kept locked in the safe and picked two at random. I wrote them both down on separate pieces of paper and folded the pages four times until they looked like blood-engorged ticks ready to pop.

"Why you making ME pick, Chase?"

"Just do it, Dollface."

"No, not until you tell me why."

I sighed and tacked on an eyeroll.

"Wait. I get it. You don't wanna know where we're going, do you?"

"Good girl. The less I know, the better. We'll meet back here in two days. The morning after the full moon. Say 'round eight?"

"Seven. Make it seven, Chase."

"Ok. Meet here at seven."

"Not a second later. Look, be careful, you big lug. Do that for me?"

I touched a plastic cheek. It felt wet. She pulled me into a tight embrace. We stood in each other's arms for a long minute. I'd forgotten how warm her body felt against mine. I made a note to re-think my single guys live longer theory when this business was over.

"I can do that, Dollface."

"Because if somethin' happens to you, Chase, I don't get paid."

Little did Dollface know, I stuffed the rest of Sorciere's retainer in her travel bag while she used the little girl's room. We were square. Paid in full.

"You should go. Can I walk you down?"

"Sure, Chase."

Outside, Nitti sat on the hood of his car smoking a cigarette despite the pouring rain. He'd offered to give Dollface a lift to Olive's apartment so she wouldn't drown in the rising water. It sounded like a good idea at the time. But I missed something—two somethings—as he opened the door for Dollface moments after we said our last goodbye.

"Don't worry, Chase. She'll get there safe and sound."

"Promise me, Nitti. I'll find you—"

"On my honor, Chase. Trust me."

Nitti smiled like a kindergartener on class photo day.

With my heart on my sleeve and my brains scrambled like a schoolboy with a crush on a teacher, I missed it. I never noticed Nitti's missing shiny gold tooth.

That wasn't The Wheel.

And I'd just sent Dollface off with him.

No Good Deed

As soon as the rain let up and the flood water receded enough to walk and not swim through the streets, I went back out to look for Tommy. Everything else could wait. I headed to Hong and Dong. I didn't question anyone because there was no one left alive to question. The Messieurs Hong and Dong had drowned in their respective offices—even though I couldn't find a drop of water in the place. Dry as a bone.

The figure slumped over the desk with the personalized, professional-looking "Mr. Ronald J. Moser" placard looked like he'd slept under water several days. His clothes were dry, but his curly hair dripped water onto the desk.

I turned out the dead guy's file drawers, which proved a dead end. For an insurance man, the late Mr. Moser kept a sparse amount of paperwork. Patience proved prudent. I struck gold and found documents related to *The Raven's Claw* mixed in with another claim. I perused the documents and got a shock. Moser declared Popeye dead and released *The Raven's Claw* seven months ago. His signature at the bottom of the doc looked as though Moser scrawled it in blood.

The dame played me.

I stormed out of the Hong and Dong offices infuriated and confused. This case was never about *The Raven's Claw* or a vacation on a private island. It fit into the larger puzzle somehow, but I couldn't stick it together. The pieces still didn't fit.

I took a few steps, and something caught my eye. My legs gave out and fell into Tommy's lifeless body. His head faced the wrong direction. I stared at the back of his head when I should've been face to face with the front. What I saw confirmed my suspicions about the kid—the back of his head housed a pair of cloudy eyes Tommy hid under an oversized ball cap.

Damn kid. Even with eyes in the back of your head, they got you.

Back at the office, I sank into my chair and raised a glass to the fallen newsie. I'd done all I could do, so I drowned myself in moonshine. My plan worked like aces. Soon I slipped into a stupor, followed by a long overdue sleep. If I dreamt about anything, I didn't remember. A small consolation prize from the guy upstairs.

With my mind rolling over the tangled web I'd tripped into, I failed to notice the blinking red message light on the phone machine.

Voice from the Big Beyond

I played and replayed the message, hoping I'd missed something the first dozen times. My pulse quickened with each new listen.

Chase. It's me. I don't think... it's crazy, but... Nitti isn't Nitti. *Like Sorciere isn't* Sorciere. *There are two of 'em. I never made it to Olive Oyl's place. He took me to the cannery. Chase, I'm frightened. The smell. I can't stand it. I think there's... no, no! Please. Don't. NO! CHASE! N O! CH—*

It ended there.

I shook off the booze, grabbed both .38s and as many rounds as I could carry. Dollface had returned the loaner to the safe before she left. Below the spare piece lay a white envelope with my name on it.

Dollface played postal and hand delivered it. The writing was hers. I'd recognize it anywhere. I couldn't bring myself to open it, so I tucked it into the top drawer of my desk and made a note to read it in two days when this was over—if me and my gills were still breathing.

I took a hit of spinach and headed for the cannery. I might be too late to save Dollface, but I'd seize the opportunity to dole out a dose of private justice.

The Hits Keep Coming

I spotted Nitti's car two blocks from the cannery parked in an alley behind Lee's Cantonese. Queer. Same alley Friedman lost his head. I drew a .38 and skulked to the car.

The smell of decay wafting out of the trunk punched my nose. I couldn't be sure, but I suspected a dead body lay stashed in the back of Netti's car. Or else the foul fumes originated at Lee's dingy take-out joint. I visited Lee's last week. I hoped for a stiff.

I jimmied the trunk. It creaked open like a coffin. It contained not a stiff, but two. A doubleheader. Don Santino and The Wheel. A look of fear frozen to the don's face. The state of rot and general putridness of the deceased gentlemen told me Santino departed this world at least a week ago. Nitti appeared fresher.

I sat with the don yesterday and took a ride with The Wheel. Someone else wore Nitti's face when they picked up Dollface. It slipped my mind to check on Miss Oyl. I made a note.

Sorciere. Popeye. Nitti. Don Santino. All had almost flawless doppelgängers. How many more were out there walking the streets of

Sweethaven alongside the monks? A question I'd explore at a later hour.

I tapped the trunk closed and crept around to the loading dock. My footsteps sounded loud. Too loud. I got the feeling someone was tailing me. Got the drop. I kept the .38 at the ready and grabbed a handful of dirt. I pointed the barrel dead ahead as a thin shadow emerged from a cover of darkness. The trigger clicked. I steadied my hand.

"Who goes there? Announce yourself!"

"Oh, don't shoot, Detective Chase!"

I recognized the squeaky voice.

"It's me. Olive! Olive Oyl!"

When she stepped into the dim light, I confirmed her identity and eased on the .38.

"Olive? What're you doing here?"

"I got this note. From your secretary."

She handed it over.

"Dollface?"

"Yeah, she told me to meet her at the cannery. Something came up, and we could leave for the safe house from here. So... here I am."

The dame giggled. It sounded like a bird call.

I looked over the note. It was all wrong. The handwriting.

"Dollface didn't write this."

"Who did?"

"I'm guessing whoever is inside the cannery. Stay close behind me. If there's any shooting, duck out fast and hitch a ride to the safe house. You got me?"

"Gotcha."

She giggled again. It grated on me. Again.

"Come on. And be quiet."

"Oh, I can be quiet, Detective Chase!"

Olive ended her declaration with—you guessed it—a giggle.

I glanced over my shoulder, making sure the broad hadn't gotten lost. It'd grown more difficult to find the ideal vantage point for watching my back since the gills came into my life. But I found the dame keeping up.

I heard a snap and rounded. Olive wore a surprised look. Her hands flew to silence her mouth, and her eyes pointed to the ground—and the branch that sounded like a landmine she'd stepped on. I tapped an index finger on my lips. The dame nodded. I crept forward. I stopped for a second when I heard the faint chanting sounds coming from inside the cannery. The closer we got to the loading dock's rolling doors, the louder the chanting.

I spied a window and pointed it out to Olive. She nodded and kept a cool distance. I hugged the wall and stole a look inside. Hooded monks, six dozen or more, gathered in a circle, chanting around a substantial hole in the ground that looked as though the one-eyed sailor had punched his way out from under the ground. A shimmering green light cast an ominous glow. There wasn't a shadow in the place as far as my eye could see.

I got down low and resumed course for the loading dock doors. The cargo doors were locked, but I found the office door ajar. I moved through the office with Olive in tow. The cannery's belly was a short walk down a stairwell. I took each step one by one, careful not to make a sound. I wasn't worried about Olive on the stairs. The dame weighed about ninety pounds carrying a bag of lemons.

On the ground floor, I crept behind a stack of crates. Beneath and beside me, the sea flowed. I reckoned this side of receiving was reserved for cargo ships, not trucks and vans. The green glow of the water unnerved me. The glow seemed brighter in the cannery. Sweethaven gave off an iridescent emerald glow, but here, in the cannery, the glow and the green shone the strongest.

I dipped my hand into the water. It felt warm. In the extended absence of sunlight, I expected it to feel frigid. I leaned to get a closer look. See what it was beneath the surface of the water. What lived below the cannery.

I stopped as soon as I heard Dollface's voice.

"Oh, Chase. Why can't you just say you love me?"

I raised my head, greeted by the sight of Olive Oyl grinning like Jack stealing the golden fiddle and pointing the barrel of a small revolver at my head. Her lips moved, but the voice wasn't hers. It belonged to Dollface.

"You were right, Chase."

I raised my hands over my head and sat up. I should've realized this was an imposter when I saw Olive came empty-handed. No travel bag in tow.

"Yeah. About what?"

"I got myself one. Helluva. Dick."

The dame first spoke as Nitti, and then ended with a rendition of Don Santino.

"Da best in Sweethaven."

What happened next happened so fast. I went to dodge behind a stack of crates, but I misjudged the weight of my gills. I flopped onto the ground like a fish out of water. The dame had a perfect shot at my back, and she took it. She fired four rounds. Three of the slugs hit their intended target, and I heard the fourth sail through the green water.

As the pain ricocheted through my body, the dame laughed. It slipped into a full-on, hair-raising cackle. I can only describe the cackle as fiendish and malevolent. I conjured an image of a witch. A hag. The kind you hear in the movies.

"Say hello to Mr. Jimmy, Detective Chase."

This voice belonged to Sorciere.

I faded to black as the sensation of water surrounded me. My body sank beneath the surface, and I fell into sleep.

Call Me Sometime, Would Ya?

The dream never changed—

I stood at the end of the pier, staring into the glowing water before me. A colossal shadow swam through the water until it stopped just off the docks and was less than fifty feet from where I stood. In my head, the sound of music enchanted my senses. A repeating, haunted melody. This was its call. The call of The Eldritch.

Around me, the people of Sweethaven gathered in neat packs. Chanting. The words finally clear to me, no longer the confused sound of an unknown language.

Arise, oh, Old One! Arise! Awaken, and take back what is yours! Awaken, Eldritch.

Then, one by one, the villagers plunged into the sea as a giant mouth breached the surface and devoured them all. I was the last to throw myself into the belly of the beast. As I passed through its teeth and slid onto a slimy slab of meat in its mouth, Sweethaven and the world beyond sank into a green darkness.

Gill-Man

I lost count of how many times I jumped into its mouth before I came to on the other side of Sweethaven. I drifted on the current and washed up on the shore under the boardwalk. Despite taking three slugs to the back and falling into the sea face-down, this dick still stood at attention. And breathing thanks to the gills.

Those anomalies saved my life and kept me breathing instead of drowning. Taking a bullet to my thin back, let alone three, would've iced me a week ago. But the gills added a protective layer over my vital parts. I rummaged through my pockets but found no spinach. Must have washed out while I was playing the floater.

I waited until I'd reverted to a mouth breather and climbed onto the boardwalk. A few hundred of my closest friends gathered to greet me. It looked as though the entire village, minus me and Popeye, converted to Eldritch. They'd all changed. A thousand human-fish hybrids' eyes stared back at me.

Clad in matching brown burlap, the sea of fresh converts lumbered toward the docks surrounding the cannery, chanting in perfect unison with every step...

... just like in my dream.

Regroup

The suspect list had thinned. Don Santino and The Wheel had passed on to the great gelato factory in the sky. If power was the motive, who stood to gain the most with the last don and his right-hand man whacked? The ten-thousand-dollar question.

I made my way back to the office. No place like home. Dollface's letter sat on my desk where I left it, daring me to read it. I tucked it back into the safe. I didn't need the distraction, not when I knew the answer was within my reach. And inching closer.

I rearranged the puzzle pieces in my mind, going over them again and again. They told an interesting story, but it wasn't whole. I remembered what Lipschitz said before the beast popped off his head like a dandelion flower from the stem. The guy seemed paranoid. In a frenzied state of mind. He was on the run, but who was it lurking in the shadows hunting him down? My eyes said Popeye, but my gut told me to look again.

I took Leo's advice and skimmed Artie Asher's journal. I commended the guy on the neatness of his penmanship before he lost his marbles. My inner green-eyed monster flared as I admired the exactness of each letter.

Asher had been looking forward to the "expedition". They sold it as a treasure hunt, which explained how Popeye got mixed up with the voyage—*he had a sixth sense for finding lost treasure.*

Lie #1: The Raven's Claw's maiden voyage was no pleasure cruise.

The scientists and sailors did not mingle. Once *The Raven's Claw* left port, the scientists never came above deck. They worked all day and into the night in a make-shift lab they fashioned out of the ship's recreation room. Asher caught glimpses of the equipment on the occasion he delivered meals or collected dirty dishes. He wrote that he'd never seen electronic gadgets and machines the likes of those before. He identified a kind of radar or sonar machine among the devices, but couldn't make heads or tails of the rest.

One scientist, Dr. Friedman, kept to himself. He sat in a corner, huddled under a reading lamp, hunched over a book. Judging by the fragile pages, Asher deduced the book was old. Perhaps ancient if the strange writing and symbols offered any clue.

Asher found one repeating symbol in the book and copied it into his journal. I knew it right away because I'd seen it all over Sweethaven in the last forty-eight hours. A circle made of tentacles with octopus eyes in the center. Artie transcribed several words and phrases he'd spied doing his job. One word stood out—"Eldritch".

Lie #2: They went out looking for something, something specific. Whatever it was, the object was connected to the Old One. But how?

The sailors knew the destination. They'd been prepared for the cold and ice. By design, *The Raven's Claw* cut through the ice with ease. Everything about the vessel told Asher the ship was forged for a single purpose—Arctic exploration.

Lie #3: The destination. The Raven's Claw set sail for the Arctic Circle, as planned. What did they hope to find up there in the frozen wasteland?

Popeye led them to the object. Excavating it from the ice was the hard part. The scientists offered little help, wearing heavy suits that resembled anti-radiation gear. The unearthed object excited them. They brought some of their gadgets topside, but kept a healthy distance—like they knew more than they said. Artie wrote about the way they immatured around it—giggling like cadets, whispering, slapping palms.

On the return voyage, Mr. Desmer Sorciere, the expedition's money, stabbed Popeye in the back and pushed him overboard into the frigid water.

Lie #4: A man financed the find and retrieve project. The dame that promised I'd never work another day in my life stayed on land for the cherry-bursting voyage. Who the hell was the broad? Wife? Sister? Mistress? Or did Desmer belong to the second Sorciere that paid my office a visit yesterday morning? Were the three of them in cahoots committing insurance fraud?

Once back on dry land, the rest of the pages grew illegible. More drawings. The symbol mostly, but I recognized some of the other scenes Asher put to paper. They were things I'd seen in my dream. Only, I noticed there was something else in the tableaus that hadn't been in my dream. Tentacles. They slithered out of the dark sea, reaching for Sweethaven.

I tucked the photo into my wallet and tossed the journal onto my desk. It sank into the mountain of paperwork. Artie confirmed much of what I already knew, but I suspected it was the tip of the iceberg. What hadn't Asher recorded in his journal? The moon would be full tomorrow. I had less than twenty-two hours to crack the case wide open.

Only one place left to visit. Arkham Asylum.

The Mad Hatter

8:32 AM – DAY 3

The Arkham Asylum for the Criminally Insane and Nervous Women opened at eight, but I felt like my gear got jammed in neutral. My feet dragged. I closed my eyes for a few hours last night, but I did not allow sleep to creep in. Sleep meant dreaming and dreaming meant I'd hear The Eldritch's call on repeat.

I passed. Every time I felt drowsy on the verge of surrendering to the sandman, I burned my arm with a match. I prayed I had enough arm and matches to make it through the night. Turned out, I did.

I arrived at Arkham thirty-two minutes after their doors opened. The place looked like a ghost town. No one sat behind the glass window at the check-in desk. No nurses or doctors on rounds. Not a single visitor. I got the feeling the staff went off and joined The Eldritch cult. Sometime yesterday too, by the look of the register behind the reception desk. The sign-in book sat open to yesterday morning, with plenty of space left on its pages.

I found Artie's name and room number. 2-023. The floor map told me Artie's room lay at the rear end of the second floor. I found it with ease and a pack of rats were the only other living beings I crossed. They scurried into the stairwell, scratching their way into the walls. Their glowing green eyes followed me in the dark until the rats disappeared in the maze behind the walls.

The deeper into the asylum I moved, I grew aware that the patients remained locked behind their room doors. The staff had fled in a hurry, but they left their charges behind to die in their rooms. Releasing them into the wild seemed the humane thing to do, but I worried how dozens of Sweethaven's criminally insane would fare. I made a note to consider my options after Artie and I had a little chat.

The control room sat in the middle of the floor connected to four long corridors. A series of small television monitors flashed static on their dusty screens while a panel of multi-colored blinking lights lit the room like a Christmas tree. The corridors showed no signs of life. The occasional groans and chants from behind the locked doors spilled into the halls, providing an eerie soundtrack.

Four silver keys stuck out of four large holes at the top of the control panel. They were labeled: Security Door 2A, 2B, 2C, 2D. The left of each key was the locked position, delineated by faded etching, while the right opened the designated security door.

The patients waited behind each heavy locked door. For a split second, I longed for the rats. Arkham had a reputation, and not a good one. Once you went in, you never got out. Experiments. Inhumane treatment. Murder. Sexual assault. And the lengthy list stretched to the floor.

The doors remained open thanks to kickbacks and bribes to Mayor Ichabod Itchybottom. I wondered if the crooked mayor's day of reckoning arrived as an Old One.

I located room 023 on a floor plan taped to the two-way observation glass and turned the key to door 2B. The thick iron door swung open. I grabbed Artie's room key and rambled down the corridor. Overhead, amber Edison bulbs flickered inside heavy-looking industrial enclosures. Shadows swirled with every step, appearing like primitive cave-drawings. The patients in Artie's wing grew restless and louder with each step. I picked the word "Eldritch" out of the monotonous meditation.

Artie's room was the third door on the left. I raised a fist to knock but thought better of it. No sense rattling cages. By now, after months locked in Arkham, Asher might be more monster than man. I slipped the rusted key into the keyhole and the door clicked open. I readied a .38 just in case the guy made a move.

I tugged at the handle and pulled the door open. Darkness crawled into the corridor, devouring the shadows. I opened the door a hair more. Not a single light shone in Artie's room. For all I could see, the guy might've already made the great escape. I didn't like it, but opening the door was the only way to see every corner of the tiny room. The warm amber glow cleared a path through the back, and there I found Artie Asher cowering under his cot.

"Artie?"

I knew he was Asher, but did Asher know?

He whispered something. A phrase. I couldn't catch a word and stepped into the room, aware my shadow blocked some of the light thrown off the Edison bulbs. I didn't see a better option than getting up close and personal.

"Hey, Asher. You in there?"

Artie laughed, a high-pitched frenzied sound that reminded me of warning sounds animals make in the wild just before pouncing. His eyes must've been sealed shut when I'd opened the door, because now a pair of glowing green eyes sized me up from inside a blanket of darkness.

"Artie?"

He laughed again and slid one arm and then the other out from under the cot, grabbing onto the floor as though his hands were suction cups.

"Artie... is dead."

Asher poked out his head and dragged his shoulders, followed by his puffy chest, into the open.

"You can call me... The Mad Hatter. I'm so glad you came."

The thing that once was Artie Asher sprang out from the darkness.

The Mad Hatter prepared to lunge—

at me!

The Split

The Mad Hatter went for the door, flying over my crouched body with grace and ease. He rolled into a ball, flipped onto his feet, and bolted for the security door. I took no chances walking into a patient wing in one of the most notorious hospitals in the state. I'd triple-checked the security door locked shut behind me.

Asher headed for a dead end.

The crash was spectacular. The door shook and groaned.

The Mad Hatter rubbed at his head. A thin stream of blood dribbled down his forehead. If this moment had been a cartoon, there'd be a mobile of chirping birds circling Artie's bruised melon.

"Ouchie!"

"Yeah, ouchie."

I sauntered to the door. Artie glimpsed blood on his fingers. His face paled, and I wondered if The Mad Hatter had ever laid eyes on the red stuff. Looking at the splayed body in front of me, and remembering the guy described in the stories I'd been told by our mutual friend, I concluded The Mad Hatter and Artie were two separate identities in one body.

Two.

I held Artie's journal and the photo up to The Hatter's crazed eyes. "Tell me about this picture, Artie."

The Mad Hatter laughed like a jester and played peek-a-boo with his hands.

"All circuits busy. Try your call again later. Please hang up."

I didn't want to shake it out of him, but if that's what it took...

I seized the back of The Hatter's head and smacked it into the photo.

"Get me Artie Asher. Now."

The Hatter grunted and squealed. Artie nowhere in sight.

Then it came to me.

This will help with your problem.

Popeye. The spinach. My gills.

I dipped a hand into my front pockets and found nothing but lint, though I still managed to excavate a few dried-out leaves with my thumb and index fingers. I must have tucked some spinach there for an emergency and forgot about it. I had no idea where the rest of it went, but I only needed a small hit.

In one brash moment, I tilted Artie's head back and threw the spinach into the back of his throat. The Hatter gagged and attempted to cough it out. I used my hand to wall up his open mouth. It didn't go down with ease, but the spinach made its way to the intended destination.

I stepped back and observed. Like something out of Robert Louis Stevenson, The Mad Hatter slipped into sleep and Artie Asher woke from his long coma. His eyes cleared like a summer storm blowing over. And when his gaze found me, Artie squinted. A glimmer of recognition shone behind his eyes.

"Detective Chase M. Down?"

I nodded.

"Welcome back, Artie Asher."

Artie surveyed the digs.

"Wh-where... am I, Chase?"

"Arkham."

"What happened to me?

"Later. Tell me everything you remember about this photo."

I waved the photo in front of his face.

Artie's expression sank. No words could ever convey the look of horror and fear that I saw overtake him.

He grabbed my shoulder and pulled me to him with a brute force I hadn't expected. Asher whispered in my ear as though we were attending a funeral and not shooting the breeze in a hospital for the criminally insane.

"We're too late. It's started, hasn't it?"

"What? Has what started, Artie?"

"The Awakening."

Lenticular

10:03 AM – Day 3

"The trip was cursed. I never shoulda taken the job. I had that feeling. You know the one, Chase? The fire in your belly."

I nodded and motioned for Artie to continue, and at a quicker pace.

"Okay. We found it in the ice. Up in the Arctic. Who knows how long it slept there? It's still asleep, I think. The ceremony needs to be done on the night of the—"

"Full moon."

We said it at the same time.

"That's tonight."

"What did you unearth up there, Artie?"

"Something terrible. There ain't enough Hail Marys out there to redeem my soul, Chase."

"Tell me what you brought to Sweethaven."

My patience thinned.

Artie grabbed the photo and pushed it in front of my eyes.

"Look again. Tell me what YOU see, Private Eye."

I tore it from his hand and moved it back enough so the photo came into focus.

"I spy... you, Leo. Friedman."

"Yes, Chase. The whole gang was there. What ELSE do you see?"

I looked harder.

"I don't know, Artie. Nothing. It's *The Raven's Claw*. A guy who doesn't want to be photographed wearing a talisman I've seen dangling around a different neck."

"No, look... again."

I zeroed in on the two scientists from the expedition that, as far as I knew, still breathed. The fake Popeye hadn't gotten around to taking care of them.

I sighed but moved my eyes to the photo one last time. Once I'd spied the obvious—crew, the money, the ship's name—I saw it. I wondered how I'd missed it earlier.

"You see it, don't you, Chase?"

I tilted the photo to the left just enough for the lenticular lens to reveal the second photo concealed beneath.

"My god, Artie. What have you done?"

"I've killed everyone."

There, under the glowing green sea surrounding Sweethaven, The Eldritch slept, snagged in a giant fishing net. A long, lone tentacle reached out of the net, worming on the stern of Sorciere's ship.

"Come on. Get up."

I pulled Asher by the neck.

"Where are you taking me, Chase?"

"My office."

The guy turned a brighter shade of pale.

"You're going to tell me how we kill this thing, Artie."

On the way out, Asher hit one big, blinking red button. And just like that, the residents of Arkham Asylum for the Criminally Insane and Nervous Women descended on Sweethaven.

Staring into the Abyss

Sweethaven resembled a ghost town, minus tumble weeds dancing in the wind. Hard to dance in the freezing rain. Save for Artie, me, and the rats, nothing living stalked the streets. We had the entire village to ourselves. I tapped the .38s for reassurance. You never know—especially in Sweethaven. Plus, the horde of Arkham's finest skulked in every shadow, behind every corner.

Artie talked in circles. Endless streams of consciousness. I never knew if I was talking to The Mad Hatter or Artie Asher. I decided it didn't matter as long as I got the intel I needed. Turned out, two heads were better than one.

"Everything changed when we reached the Arctic."

"How so?"

Artie growled like a cornered stray.

"It just did, okay? It was all hurry up, do this now. No food. No rest. Just... faster! Faster! FASTER! FASTER! FASTER!"

The words shot out like rockets. The guy foamed at the mouth. Asher looked like he needed to be taken out to the shed in the woods and put down. The Mad Hatter. I tapped his shoulder, hoping it'd send The Hatter packing.

Right now, I needed Artie Asher. Later, I knew I'd need The Hatter. And Popeye.

"When we found it... I felt its power."

I felt it too. Back at the cannery, like a blast wave following an A-bomb.

"It got in while we slept. Didn't matter if we closed our eyes for a minute or three hours. It got in. Infected us. I felt its tentacles reach inside and poison me. I dreamt the same dream over and over again. Every time I closed my eyes, it was there. Do you dream, Chase?"

"I do."

His eyes cleared, and Artie checked back in.

"You've heard its call. You've been touched."

Asher indicated the gills.

"Even asleep, the thing gave off an energy. Bad mojo. I watched the sun disappear behind clouds that had no business being there. And then it rained. Once it started—"

"It never stopped," we both said at the same time.

"You remember what the sun looks like, Chase? You remember the last time you saw it? Felt it?"

I shook my head.

Artie looked to the dark heavens. He raised his arms to the sky and bathed in the hard rain. I watched his eyes close as his mouth turned into a gigantic grin. For a moment, Asher looked more like a guy getting his first kiss than a half-crazed sailor and part-time goon for hire.

"Neither do I. Neither... do... I."

"What's happening in Sweethaven?"

"You ever look into the abyss, Chase? Peer into the darkness and see if anything stares back?"

I felt eyes on me. Was it the abyss reaching out to me?

"In my line of work, you learn to make darkness your friend."

Artie opened his eyes and craned his head in my direction.

"Yeah, I see the darkness around you. It's had a taste of you. Now, it'll never let you go. Everything you touch will be infected, Chase. You're damned. Like all of us on that ghost ship. Like everyone in Sweethaven. The end starts here. The village will finally be known for something. Isn't that ironic?"

"Artie—"

"It followed us here. Endless night. A world of never-ending rain. It's devouring everything. Erasing it. You don't remember your fifth birthday, do you? Getting your diploma? Popping your cherry? Any of it ring bells?"

He had me there. The photo album in my mind went blank past a certain point. I remembered next to nothing about my life before The Eldritch moved into the cannery.

"It's not strong enough to spread across the world. When it wakes up and it brings some friends from the other side? The world will become its church and we'll be either its worshippers or its servants. How does it feel to be damned, Chase?"

"There's always been a target on my back. There has to be a way to stop it."

Artie laughed and shook his head.

"You can't kill the infinite, Chase."

"Put it back to sleep then? Come on, Artie. You must've heard something. Anything that'll help. It must be vulnerable sometime, or else why need an army of cultists?"

"It likes being worshipped."

The Eldritch sounded more like a politician than an ancient god.

"But I did overhear something. One time when they thought I was above deck."

Asher cut off. I wanted to throttle him, but knew he needed to tell the story at his pace. It took all my resolve to keep my hands tucked in my pockets and not bash his head with the butt of my .38.

"An incantation. It was in a book. Older than the Bible from the look of it. The language was strange, but somehow, I could understand every word. I only got a peek inside, but..."

I urged him on.

"But I think I saw the invocation to put it back to sleep."

"Did you write it down, Artie? Please tell me you wrote it down."

He shook his head. My stomach dropped.

"I memorized it."

Chatterbox

Back at the office, Artie Asher talked himself into a delirium. I locked the front door and slid Dollface's chair under the handles. But a flimsy door wouldn't be enough to keep out The Eldritch's long tentacles if they came knocking.

According to Artie, we still had time to stop it. A few hours. The moon rose in Sweethaven at 6:50 PM. The clock ticked faster than ever.

I leaned back in my chair, hoping it would hold, and eyed Artie lounging on the couch. His foamy lips still flapped a mile a minute as his physique changed before my eyes. I reasoned since he'd switched back to the Artie body, the thing poisoning him—and us—could finish what it started in the Arctic.

My temples throbbed. I fished the extra aspirins I pocketed at the coffee shop and swallowed them dry. I turned to Asher and prepared to file a noise complaint when he finally said something interesting.

"... always touching that ugly necklace around his neck. He acted like we all had our eye on it, like we were going to pocket it or something."

"What did it look like?"

"The necklace? Ugly thing. It kinda looked like a giant squid. The tentacles wrapped around its head, and it had these two glowing green eyes. When we hit the Arctic, I felt like them eyes were always on me. They glowed like green light houses."

Artie sketched the symbol in his journal. How'd I miss the connection? That symbol connected everything, and that necklace — it *was a necklace, after all* — connected Sorciere and the mysterious guy on deck. Did the necklaces come in a matching set — his and *hers?* The pieces were falling into place. The picture becoming clearer. I could almost make it out.

"He was always on deck smoking those fancy French cigarettes like he was better than us 'cause he was smoking imported cigs."

The thought sucker punched me. *Air Frais. Fresh Air.*

I snared Artie before he raced onto something less interesting.

"Who was smoking, Artie?"

"Mr. Sorciere. Smoked like Chiminey Cricket. Come to think of it, I don't think I ever saw the guy go below deck. Ain't that queer? Even in the cold, he sat staring at it."

The whole thing felt queer. It stank.

"Think for a second, Artie. Do you remember the brand of cigarette?"

"Uhh... it'll come to me. Please hold."

I wondered how much of Artie Asher was The Mad Hatter, and how much the Hatter was him. All the while, the clock ticked.

"Oh, yeah. I got it, Chase."

I watched his lips form the words, and I knew what they'd say.

"Air Frais."

Bingo.

I readied the final question. I knew the answer, but needed Asher to confirm the suspicion.

"What happened to Popeye, Artie?"

"He... split. Split in two."

Asher hooted and, for an instant, his face switched to The Hatter.

A Door Closes

4:37 PM – Day 3

Artie's incessant chatter, coupled with the patter of the rain on the glass, lulled me to sleep. Before The Eldritch stole my dreams, I thought about Dollface and her uncertain fate. I dared not return to the cannery without a solid plan to send the ancient god back to the abyss. I prayed she was out there kicking up a fuss.

The darkest of shadows covered the office and Asher went mute. An alarm bell went off somewhere in my head. I shot upright, a .38 at the ready. False alarm. Artie peered through the dusty blinds.

"Closer now. Can't you feel it, Chase?"

I did, but I wasn't sharing my feelings with a semi-psychotic.

"It's calling to US. Calling... calling... callinggggg..."

Artie's voice trailed off. I gathered my meager supplies—two loaded .38s, spare cartridges, Artie's journal, and the lenticular photo. Something nagged me about the photo, but I didn't know what. It'd come to me. It always did.

Before I clicked off the office lights, I took one last look at the dump I'd called home for the last twelve years. I hoped something would stir, but I came up empty in the feelings department. Without Dollface, the office was nothing but rooms fashioned out of wood.

If I was lucky, I'd still be alive in the morning. Then, I'd return to collect Dollface's note from the safe and finally get out of Sweethaven, and never look back.

It was a big "if".

I flicked the switch, and the office went dark.

As I descended the stairs, I glanced back one last time at Down Investigations and tipped my hat.

Goodnight, my sweet. 'Til we meet again.

Shit Happens

We cut through the backstreets and alleyways. Force of habit. The cannery was a ten-minute walk from the office. Fifteen if you window shopped. I had one stop to make. Shitface's place sat at the halfway mark. I planned to make an unannounced visit. Inquire about Mr. Sorciere. Then, head straight for the cannery and the lot of cultists.

I kept us at an even pace. Artie fell behind, sliding into a trance-like state. A snap of the fingers or a quick whistle roused him, but I wondered how deep he'd slip the closer we got to The Eldritch's nest. The call grew stronger with every step.

Everywhere I turned, shadows moved in the night. Their slithering, sloppy noises chilled my blood. I didn't need eyes on them to know we weren't the only ones answering the call. The Eldritch convoked its brethren on the other side. Soon, the one world would overtake the other.

How I knew this? I can't say. Just a feeling. Something out of a dream.

The path to Shitface's pad proved easy. The sight I stumbled onto? Less so.

Someone decided it was a good day to flush Shitface down his own toilet—shit face first. About half his head fit into the bowl. For once, being full of shit proved helpful. Bits of him spilled over the sides.

The floor drowned in a brown river. I laughed. Shitface had flipped his killer a shitty middle finger.

RIP, Shitface.

Wherever it is turds go when they're flushed, I hope there's two-ply.

Burnin' for You

For the two Sorcieres, I was on my own. Nothing but dead ends. I had enough to see the picture, but it remained out of focus. In time, all the pieces would slide into place and the full canvas would reveal itself. Time. An asset running out.

The docks came into view. The cannery rose out of the shadows directly behind, eclipsing the docks. I never noticed before, but the cannery resembled a medieval fortress. My resolve waned, but my feet kept walking.

Insanity overtook Artie. I saw him slipping away with each step. The Mad Hatter slept for now. I didn't want to wrangle with The Hatter until necessary. I grabbed Asher's arm and steered him through the docks like he was one of those novelty talking dummies. Words turned to gibberish several blocks ago. I could find more uses for a bowl of jelly than Artie Asher in his current form. Lucky for both of us, he spilled everything he knew before parting with his sanity.

We'd almost cleared the docks when I saw *The Raven's Claw* anchored at the end of the longest pier in Sweethaven. I wondered how I missed it before. The massive ship stood out like a Catholic nun turning tricks in a house of ill repute.

I tugged Artie toward the king-sized vessel. He shrieked and cowered at the sight of it, kicking and screaming. I grabbed a length of rope from a nearby docked ship and tied Asher to a post. The knot just needed to hold long enough for me to eye the ship.

I moved down the pier, careful to mind my surroundings. With the full moon little more than an hour away, anything could leap from the dark. No use taking chances. The .38s sat at the ready, waiting to be called into action.

The Raven's Claw bobbed feet away. And that's when I heard a familiar voice.

"Well, hello, Detective Chase."

Chase, not Down. First Sorciere.

I eyed The Eldritch charm dangling around her neck.

"What took you so long to find me? Another dick that failed to measure up. I hoped for better from you."

"I live to disappoint. Why don't you let me come aboard, and we can talk about it?"

No point bringing up the rest of the dough. She never planned on paying that invoice.

"Oh, I bet you have questions. But I'm all out of answers, you see."

I tugged at one of the ship's ropes lassoed to a post.

"Come on, Sorciere. Let me up."

"Oh, Detective. I wish I could grant you more time, especially in this moment. But I'm just one big mothah—"

Dollface?

Sorciere straightened her back. Her eyes danced about wildly. A confused, frightened look swept over her face. My hand flew to a .38. Something felt wrong. The scene wasn't right.

Her face eased back into its usual holier than thou disguise. Behind it all, the true face hid. The talisman pulsed green. It shot in all directions, tinting the dark.

"It's been fun, Chase. See ya on... the othah... side."

I pulled the gun just as *The Raven's Claw* exploded. Shockwaves threw me into the water. I ducked below the surface, mindful of falling debris, and swam to the shore. Artie rambled on as though he stood at the pulpit of a packed cathedral. We watched as fire devoured *The Raven's Claw*.

Last stop on the runaway train: the cannery…

…to defeat a cosmic deity and cast out the evil presence that defiled Sweethaven.

The sea swallowed the remnants of the ship. A heavy cloud of black smoke rose from the green sea—a cloud in the shape of not a raven, but a vulture.

The Bad Moon Rises

One hour to moonrise.

I gagged Artie's mouth with a handkerchief. No reason to announce our arrival, though I'd bet our hunting party was expected. Asher resisted the muzzle, but settled as the reality of the situation and what we were about to do dawned on him.

"I'm going 'round to get a look."

The words came out just above a whisper, but Artie acknowledged them.

I lost sight of Sweethaven in the mist and fog that swarmed the cannery. Artie also disappeared into the stuff. He let out a small moan every now and again to let me know he hadn't been dragged off to the netherworld.

I felt surrounded, but the cultists remained obscured by the fog. The Eldritch sent a welcoming party. How nice. Now that a surprise entrance was off the table, it didn't matter how we got into the cannery.

Hurried footfalls came at me from all directions. Artie's signal groans ceased. I drew both revolvers. Footsteps closed in. I pulled both hammers back and armed the .38s. I'd put some lead into anything that stepped out of the fog. I dug in and stood my ground, moving in a circle to cover myself since I did not get eyes in the back of my head.

The fog rolled in. Total whiteout. Footsteps. Running. Cultists getting closer. Beside me. Behind me. Coming from the left. Then from my right. I fired into the swirling mist.

BANG! BANG! Thud. BANG! BANG! BANG! Thud. BANG! BANG! BANG! Thud.

I emptied both cartridges into the fog. Several hit the bull's eye. I moved fast. Double-time like in the service. I braced, expecting a slug to the back any second. I dodged, just not quick enough. Something hard caught the back of my head, and I went down. I felt blood roll down my back. I tasted it as the red stuff dripped into my gills. The salty-sweet taste of iron flooded my mouth.

Dozens of arms reached for me, poking out of the haze like a mass of tentacles attached to an unseen body. They caught me, grabbing me and pulling me to my feet just as the lights went out and I lost my favorite—and only—hat.

The Call

6:32 PM – Day 3

Eighteen minutes to moonrise.

"Poke me again, I'll serve you those fingers for dinner."

The poking ceased. I opened my eyes long enough to glance at my watch, then returned them to their shut position. Someone bent to meet my face. Their breath brushed my cheek.

"Wake up, Chase."

Artie Asher. No sign of The Hatter.

"It's gonna start soon. The Awakening. You're gonna want to see this. Be a part of it."

"Be a part of it? Artie, what's wrong with—"

I opened my eyes and jumped back. Artie's eyes, like the rest of Sweethaven, shone a luminous shade of emerald. He'd succumbed while I slept. Artie Asher answered the call.

"Jesus. Not you too, Artie."

I pushed the guy off and staggered to my feet. My hands flew to my head as though their touch could erase the headache. A burning sensation swelled in my back. Additional changes coming.

Thousands of candles illuminated the cannery. Despite their flames, the place felt colder than a morgue freezer. I struggled to focus. Nothing looked right. Green goo dripped from the ceiling, while a shimmering slime slithered across the floor. Around me, wails and screams hung in the air.

And something else. Something otherworldly—the cosmic chittering of a million creatures on the other side, where The Eldritch once lived. A million monstrosities waiting to break on through to *our* side and call it home.

The rear loading doors sat open. A giant glowing mass sat motionless in the sea. Its light glimmered with the rippling of the water. The ancient thing under the water inched closer.

It took longer than it should have for me to recognize the place. We stood on a platform at the top of the cannery, perched in what's called "the nest". Down below, my former friends and neighbors gathered to usher in their new god. Their chanting sounded like the hum of a fan on a summer's afternoon—a long, low *whirrrr*.

But I knew better. I recognized the words. Every one. Artie wrote them down for me. As I moved closer to checkmate, I prayed I memorized the incantations in the correct sequence.

Artie moseyed up beside me. With my brains still scrambled, I saw three of him standing next to me. Each wore a devilish smile.

"It's going to be magnificent, Chase. Accept the change. Heed the Call."

The three Arties tilted their heads at once and moved to whisper in my ear.

"Don't worry, Chase," the three Ashers whispered in unison, but the voices belonged to The Hatter. "We got this."

They backed away, and I got three winks for listening.

Then, something going on downstairs caught my eye. A new addition since my last visit—a giant circle painted on the floor in front of the crater. The circle resembled a wheel with Eldritch writing on the outside, and the wheel sliced into equal-sized slivers. Spokes of a wheel. And there, I spied the four missing dons and the two MIA scientists.

Don Santino remained absent. His body stuffed into the trunk of his car alongside Jimmy "The Wheel" Nitti.

The dons and scientists lay prone, each within their own spoke of the wheel—lined up like appetizers. Or... offerings.

The wheel was an altar.

Their arms and legs splayed open, tied to what looked like rusted iron spikes hammered into the floor. Don Lemone groaned. A thin line of blood dribbled down his thick, fleshy neck. The Eldritch got Don Lemone's tongue.

Got them all. The dons wagged their tongues no more.

And in the center of it all, on a raised stake that would've made Joan of Arc jealous, Miss Olive Oyl wriggled in her restraints like a worm on a fishing hook. She screamed an awful, eardrum-splitting squawk. I wanted to dash downstairs and muzzle the dame, but time ticked on.

The chanting gained steam. Movement below. The cultists. I found Flo's frightening fish transformation in the sea of oddities. The gal's coffee-slinging days were over.

Right on schedule, Mr. Desmer Sorciere stepped out of the green shadows. I spotted the talisman around his neck. A green energy swirled around the necklace's circular frame while a green pulse of light shot out of the octopus eyes in the charm's center.

"Desmer Sorciere, I presume?"

The dashing gent bowed.

"At your service, Detective. So glad you could make it."

"Wouldn't miss it for the end of the world."

Desmer Sorciere frowned, over-selling it like a silent screen actor.

"Too bad your secretary couldn't be here. Dollface, was it?"

Was?

My blood boiled. There'd be time to mourn the dead later.

Behind me, Artie whispered, "Chase…"

"I can see by your expression, I nailed it, as they say. Now, what do you say we get on with the show!"

The chanting grew louder and louder until the foundation shook. Desmer waved a hand like an orchestra conductor and the cultists dropped a few decibels. No longer deafening, the sound buzzed around my ears like a mosquito.

"Hang on a sec. What happened to Dollface?"

Desmer grinned. His entire face bubbled with fiendish delight.

"Don't you know, Detective Chase? You were there when she died."

The Raven's Claw. The fire. Sorciere. Dollface.

A piece clicked into place.

"How'd you do it? Enchanted object? Spell?"

"A wizard… never reveals how the trick was done. Only confirms that it was… done."

Dollface. Dead.

"I mean, not to belabor the point, but *you* killed her, in a way. If you'd only stayed away. Taken the money and run like I thought you and your little painted doll would do, then you never would have been on the docks tonight. And I never would have needed to take matters into my own hands."

Finally, caught on my line. I had him. Or should I say, her.

"That's in the past. Nothing to be done about it now. It's the glorious future I'm concerned with. The return of the Old One. A new age about to begin."

"Yeah, end of the world. New beginning. Blah. Blah. I've heard it all before. You're unoriginal. You're not even trying anything new. Isn't that a gas? You've unearthed something old... maybe the oldest thing in creation. I expected more from YOU, Desmer."

"Happy to disappoint, Detective."

There. His face. It glitched as though two faces squeezed into one.

"Before you kill me and everyone else in Sweethaven, do me a solid?"

Desmer sighed, but did not stir.

"What is it you want?"

"Got a smoke? You know... a last request."

Desmer sneered. His mouth moved, but the voice belonged to Dollface.

"I thought you quit, you big lug."

And then, like a magic trick in a roadside carnival, Desmer Sorciere transformed into Dollface. A near perfect clone. The look. The smell. The walk. The talk. But it lacked a soul. And had no heart.

"Have one on me," Desmer said with Dollface's voice.

The thing fished out a pack of Air Frais and handed me one.

"Air Frais. Fancy."

The thing winked and lit the cig. I took a long drag, savoring the taste of the world's most expensive poison.

"Not bad."

I emptied my lungs of smoke and stole a glance at my watch. 6:39 PM.

"The best."

I side-eyed Artie. He stood at the edge of the platform. His eyes fixed on the glowing mass beneath the sea. I stole up behind him.

"I've never seen anything like it, Chase. It's... beautiful."

I grabbed his hand and pressed until I broke skin.

"Not now. We're so close. Just... hang on a few minutes longer. Can you do that, Artie?"

"I don't know, Chase. I'll try."

I patted Asher's shoulder.

"I think it's time, Artie. You still got it?"

He nodded. His eyes never strayed from the sleeping god.

"Eat it. We need The Hatter."

Again, he nodded, but remained frozen in place.

"Artie. Eat it. We need The Hatter."

"Yeah, okay, Chase."

"Good man. Don't let Desmer see you eat it."

I turned, heading back to Desmer.

Artie called back.

"Hey, Chase. Thank you."

No, Artie Asher. Thank you.

I knew there'd never be a plaque or monument recognizing Artie's sacrifice, but I made a note to never forget his part in all of this. And if I failed, there'd be no one left to remember anyway.

Artie's Nosedive

6:41 PM – DAY 3

Nine minutes to moonrise.

Desmer pulled the ancient book out from under his cloak. Olive shrieked. My ears winced. Out of the corner of my eye, I caught Artie chewing. I wanted to smile, but kept my poker face on.

"Let's go down and get a closer look, shall we... Artie?"

Desmer's voice enchanted. Hell, I'd nearly fallen under its spell. But Artie... the thing in the water called to him. I knew because I heard it singing in my head, too. The only play I had left was a long game. Wait. Hope I timed everything right.

"Gooo downnnn, Arrrr-tieeee. Watch the Awakening of a god."

The call got to him. Artie nodded his head and skulked down the stairs to the main level of the cannery. He'd gone off script. Time to improvise and hope The Hatter made an appearance soon.

"Before you do the thing with the book, and you know, end the world as we know it, tell me something. What do the dons have to do with any of this?"

A twinkle flashed in Desmer's green eyes.

"Really, Detective? I thought you'd have it all figured out by now."

"I do. Most of it. I'm just missing one small piece."

Desmer lowered the book and gave me his full attention.

"By all means, Detective Chase. You have about three minutes, I believe, before I'll have to cut... you off. Thrill me."

"This case was never about a ship or a vacation on some island in the Caribbean. There were no rich clients, and *The Raven's Claw* was never grounded."

I checked on Artie. He lumbered toward the loading dock and the creature in the sea. Another minute or two. Buy me a minute or two...

"You used me."

Desmer feigned shock.

"Me, Detective?"

I advanced. Desmer held his ground.

"Yes, you. It was you that hired me. Sucked me in with promises of money. The dream of getting out of Sweethaven. You knew I'd take the case. The dough. And what did any of it amount to? A hill of beans."

Desmer indicated The Eldritch.

"Much more than that, I'd say."

"This case is about one thing—power. With the real Sorciere moving the cannery out of Sweethaven, it was anyone's game. You knew she was going to sell because you've been in negotiations for almost a year. Why? Because whoever controls the sea is king. Or... queen. But then there were the dons. They had to go or else they'd challenge you for control. Nobody likes a mob war. Too crude, too bloody."

"Two minutes, Detective. Time for the big wrap-up."

"You heard about an ancient book and a god buried in the ice. I don't know how you got wind of it, but you did. And that was the answer to all your problems. Gain absolute power. Sweethaven would be a test run to see if you could control it. So you arranged an expedition with disposable men. The bare minimum you needed to get there and back, excavate the thing—"

"That thing is a god. Show some respect."

"Excavate that THING, and the scientists to translate the text, keep the thing alive, open the gate between our world and theirs. Once you brought it back to Sweethaven, you set in motion your plan to convince the real Sorciere to sell the cannery to you by poisoning the water supply. You knew it would contaminate everything, including all the food processed at the cannery. People changed. And it never stopped raining."

Desmer sneered. "Sweethaven IS a bit like jolly old London these days."

Artie looked at me and nodded. Almost go time. I read it on his face. The Hatter was about to make his entrance.

"Now, with the cannery as good as yours, all you had to do was eliminate the competition, the dons, and silence everyone who knew about the expedition and what you unearthed. You didn't need me to prove Popeye was dead. You knew he was alive. Out there. You just needed me to keep him busy. Keep him distracted while you played the shell game. You killed Pete Peterson and—"

Tommy.

"—the newsies to keep it all quiet, because the less anyone knew about the dark happenings, the better. The less I knew. You couldn't take the chance that I'd put the pieces together before you waltzed into my office delivering your cock and bull story."

"I do hope you wrote that enthralling piece of fiction down some-place, Detective. You have quite the gift."

I nodded. I reached up to tip my hat, forgetting it fell off my head somewhere outside the cannery.

"But in your fantasy, three pieces don't fit."

I threw Desmer's words back at him. "Thrill me."

"Dead or alive, why would anyone throw Popeye overboard?"

"Anyone? You did that after you stabbed him in the back. Why, he saw the most, right? He stumbled onto the bigger plan. You underestimated the one-eyed sailor. Despite his looks, he's a smart cookie. He figured out what you dug up and what you planned to do with it. He spent the most time around it, didn't he? That's why he changed first. And you couldn't let him walk the streets of Sweethaven in his altered state. Too many questions."

"Fascinating. Truly."

"What's number two?"

"You say I hired you?"

I nodded.

"You did."

"But I've never met you until this evening. How could I have hired you when I've never even met you? A bit queer, Detective, no?"

"That got me turned upside down for a while. But we both know how you did it. And I think it's safe to say we both know WHO and WHAT you are?"

My eyes locked on Desmer, and the talisman hanging unguarded around his neck.

"Number three?"

Desmer indicated Miss Olive Oyl. "Why would anyone want to put up with this insufferable... woman?"

"That's the best part. You needed her most of all. She's the most important piece of the puzzle."

Desmer stepped in. We stood toe-to-toe.

"Needed that insignificant bug for what?"

"Bait."

"Bait?"

Check. Mate.

Artie turned and screeched. Desmer's head whipped toward the ruckus. I pulled him by his cloak and grabbed his head, forcing him to look at what was until a second ago Artie Asher.

"Desmer Sorciere... meet... The Mad Hatter."

The Hatter let out a cry. In an instant, he flew into the air. A giant leap. Heading straight for "the nest". At the same moment, I rounded on Desmer. He resisted, but I had the upper hand. Physical strength.

At least, I *had* the upper hand until my gills decided it was the perfect time for a growth spurt. I screamed. My body dragged me down, but I fought to remain standing. A shadow passed over me, and I knew The Hatter was about to pounce.

I wrapped my hands around the talisman and ripped it off Desmer's neck. The Hatter stole the ancient book. The creature held it above his head and waved it in triumph.

A second later, The Hatter took a nosedive off the platform just as the water rose like a tsunami. Tentacles reached from beneath the sea and thwacked the floor. Then two more tentacles breached the surface. And two more as The Eldritch pulled its immense body out of the water through the hole in the cannery floor.

The Old One squirmed and slithered onto the floor, sliding with ease and speed. Its monstrous mouth opened. The whole of the universe glimmered in the back of The Eldritch's throat.

Its call boomed in my head as I screamed louder. The gills tore through my flesh as they grew. My skin hardened as scales sprouted and covered my entire body. Every part of me hurt as the transformation completed.

I looked up in time to see The Mad Hatter disappear into The Eldritch's open mouth— taking the ancient spell book along for the ride.

And, just as The Hatter slipped into the abyss, he let out a deafening war cry. Seconds later, a horde of Arkham's finest stormed the cannery.

My watch read 6:50 PM. Moonrise.

The cult swarmed. Heading right for Olive, the dons, and the last two survivors of the Arctic expedition. The crazed former patients kept as many of them busy as possible. The cannery floor blurred with quick-handed action as cultists and lunatics fell in equal measure. But from where I stood, the inmates of Arkham got the upper hand.

Desmer sizzled as though someone used him for kindling. He discarded the cloak and dropped to his knees. A thousand faces swam over his, but I only recognized a few— Sorciere, Olive, Desmer, The Wheel, Santino, Pete Peterson, and Dollface.

The thing howled and bellowed. Its voice changed with every new wail. When it settled, the voice was that of an old woman. A practitioner of dark magic. A sorceress who could charm or curse objects to her will.

Exposed, she let out a hair-raising cackle. A *witch's* cackle.

She rose to her feet, and at last I saw the thing that crawled around in the skins of others. And I remembered what I'd thought of her when the real Sorciere came calling—the first one appeared haggard.

Hag-gard.

HAG.

Desmer. *Of the Sea.*

Sorciere. *Witch.*

The cult moved in. Olive screamed. Inmates from Arkham pushed back.

The Sea Hag cackled.

The Eldritch slammed its tentacles into the floor, then raised itself and walked toward the wheel.

"You can't stop it now, Detective Chase! You've lost the book!"

I groaned and grimaced as I rose to my webbed feet.

"I don't need the book."

The Eldritch whipped a tentacle and off popped Don Lemone's head. It rolled past Olive who, as you can guess, screamed. Off came Don Giovanni's head next, followed by the heads of Don Perry Gon, and Don Pedro. The altar ran red. Blood spurted and spilled. Olive got covered in the stuff. Her shabby little outfit looked as though someone had dropped a bucket of pig's blood on it.

The Eldritch wrapped a tentacle around each of the scientists and popped them into its mouth like grapes. It turned its towering body and glowing eyes to Olive Oyl, who did not scream but fainted at the sight. The Old One rose on all eight of its tentacles and tiptoed toward Popeye's passed-out paramour.

The Sea Hag shot at me, throwing me to the ground. Warts and bubbling boils festered on her slimy green face. Her foul breath repulsed me, and I flinched when she bared a set of razor-sharp teeth. Moss and seaweed dangled from her limbs. A mane of long, stringy gray hair smacked my face as I saw myself reflected in her pitch-black eyes.

She wrapped her claws around my neck, digging her long, green fingernails into my skin. They sliced through my newly minted scaly skin, drawing blood. She squeezed, choking me with a surprising force for an old hag.

I smiled and said, "I don't need the book... because... I have him..."

Then the building shook. The whole place rocked on its side as though it might tip over and fall into the sea. The Eldritch moved its eyes to the front cargo-bay doors, which were sealed shut. A clap of thunder and a flash of lightning. The doors shattered and the pieces flew into the air, taking out several cultists as they fell back down.

Outside, the rain hammered Sweethaven. Another thunderous boom. A crackle of green lightning. And there, in the doorway, stood Popeye, the sailor guy.

The Sea Hag eased on my neck, distracted by the sudden arrival of the one-eyed sailor.

Popeye reached into his pocket and pulled out a glowing green can of spinach. He tore the top open with his teeth.

"That's all I can stands..."

He threw back his head and emptied the can into his mouth, swallowing it down in several quick gulps.

"... I can't stands... no more."

Clash of the Titans

Moonrise.

"Ohhh, Popeyeeeee," Olive squealed.

Popeye crushed the tin can with ease as though it was a paper airplane. Tossing the can aside, he stepped into the cannery. The shadowy form his body cast in the moonlight grew with each step until it covered every square inch of the cannery.

The hulking shape shone in the moonlight, and a glowing green liquid coursed through his veins. The muscles in his arms inflated, growing three times their size—at least. His beefy chest puffed, cracking and rippling with solid muscle. Then Popeye arched his back. The muscles popped to mammoth proportions. The sailor's hands, which were massive at the start, swelled until I thought they might burst. An emerald flame ignited behind Popeye's nightmarish one-eye.

When Popeye told me spinach could slow the effects, he'd been telling the whole truth—but not the whole story. Spinach can slow The Old One's gruesome effects on the human body—but ONLY if the change is incomplete. That's why it helped with my gill problem but increased The Mad Hatter's madness and Popeye's size and strength. Their changes were complete. Two sides of every changed person, and the contaminated spinach strengthened the darker side.

The Eldritch's eyes flared, their green glow matching Popeye's lone eye. The ancient god clicked and chirped in a high-pitched squall that rivaled Olive Oyl. Its tentacles thrashed, sending cultists and candles flying. Screams echoed throughout the cavernous cannery as cultists caught fire. Their chants continued as their flesh sizzled and charred until immolation. The warehouse smelt like a Fourth of July barbecue.

The Sea Hag raged as Popeye lunged at The Eldritch with a thunderous roar. The Old One sank to the ground and raised four of its immense tentacles. They waved as though under the water. The cosmic creature opened its terrible beaks, shooting a toxic black cloud into the air.

The cultists gathered and closed in, chanting and exalting the ancient god. The cannery walls rose and fell as though they took a breath. On the other side, the foulest of creatures pushed and punched at the barrier. Their Awakening, and arrival, almost complete. The Eldritch clicked a welcome to its brethren, but its green eyes never lost sight of Popeye.

The Sea Hag tightened her grip on me, and I sputtered a series of gurgles and wheezes as my air supply cut off. The old witch cackled with delight, throwing her head back in ecstasy. I had one play. I threw my arms around the crone and pulled her into a tight embrace. Her eyes bulged as she fell silent. I squeezed until her grotesque face touched mine. My stomach soured as her rank breath hit my nose.

I smiled and managed a laugh as I rolled off the dizzying platform. The witch let loose a hair-raising scream as we fell to the ground below, landing a handful of feet away from Popeye and The Eldritch. I stole a look and glimpsed their wrestling figures. Popeye seized the creature by its tentacles and spun it through the air as it chirped and clicked.

My grip loosened, and the Sea Hag sat up. Her eyes homed in on mine.

"Didn't I say you'd never work another day in your life? Didn't I? Die already, Dick. Die! I fulfilled my end of our agreement. You can't work if you're dead!"

The crone cackled.

With the Hag distracted, I rolled across the cannery floor, avoiding the cultists and the growing flames, until we spilled into the searing sea. The Hag bellowed and hollered. A series of bubbles floated out of her mouth as the sea drowned out the sounds. Her eyes darted about as her talons pawed at the water like a drowning dog.

She peered down at me, horrified by the shit-eating grin on my face as I breathed under the water and the Hag drowned. Queer she never wondered how I survived the slug to the back. My hands found her neck and squeezed.

Above, on the surface, fire engulfed the cannery. The flames flickered and danced on the green water. A second later, as the Sea Hag struggled to break the grip, The Eldritch and Popeye flopped into the sea. The old god shot a rapid-fire series of black ink bullets at the one-eyed sailor, who forced the creature into the depths of the dark green waters. The clicks and chirps faded until the Hag's watery gasps were the only sound. Popeye's comically large pipe floated up from the sea's darkest depths towards the surface.

Her eyes rolled back in her head, and there came one final gasp as the Sea Hag's body went limp. I throttled her neck several more times before releasing it. The body glided away from me. The lifeless arms and legs danced like a marionette as the sea's movement animated the crone. I grabbed Popeye's pipe.

Then I sprang forward as a massive wave rushed by me. A wall of bubbles encased me. One of Popeye's burly hands latched onto me and dragged me to the surface. He threw me to the side. I rolled into a ball, traveling the length of the cannery until I crashed into a cultist.

"Popeye!"

Olive cried, a mix of relief and horror as she saw the thing Popeye had transformed into.

"Don't look at me!"

The chanting ceased as the cannery fell silent and still. Flames climbed the walls. Thick clouds of smoke exited through the open doors, getting lost in the endless sea of fog and mist.

I made my way to standing and pushed through the gawking cultists until I reached the end of the cannery. The Sea Hag lay face down in the water. The dead-man's float. I retrieved the Hag's talisman and studied it for a long moment, unaware the hulking sailor had stolen up beside me.

"I need you to untie Olive. Explain... all of this."

"I think... this belongs to you."

I slipped him the pipe. He stuck it in the corner of his mouth.

"I thanks you."

I indicated Olive Oyl with my head.

"Don't you want to do it?"

"I... can't. Not like this."

"Gotcha. What do we do with this?"

I held up the witch's talisman.

"Allow me."

Popeye grabbed it and crushed it in his palm. The talisman crackled and gave a quick burst of light before going dark. A death rattle.

"What do we—"

Before I could finish, The Eldritch sprang from the sea with a horrifying cry. A tidal wave swept through the cannery, dousing the flames. The creature made ground behind us, near the altar, waving its tentacles until they cupped into place. It rose and walked toward Popeye and me.

"Oh, Popeyeeee," Olive squealed. "Look out!"

The cultists resumed their chanting while Arkham's inmates assaulted. The cannery quaked as a host of cosmic beasties knocked at the door to our world.

Popeye grabbed another can of spinach. He tore into it and downed it. I stood in awe as his frame grew more brutish and packed with muscle. Yet, somehow, that pipe remained two sizes too large for his face.

The one-eyed sailor steeled himself, preparing to attack.

I tapped his throbbing forearm.

"Keep it busy. I just need a minute."

"Whatever you're gonna do, do's it fast."

A second later, Popeye was nothing but a blur as he propelled himself at the old god, tangling with it one last time.

"Popeye! Nooooo!"

Behind me, something burst through the wall. The creatures were coming through.

The cultists flooded the cannery, chanting with the speed of an auctioneer.

I moved to higher ground, not wanting to be crushed as the two beasts wrestled. As I bolted up the steps to the observation platform, I body-checked any cultists in my way. They fell to the ground with a messy thud.

When I reached the top, I moved to the edge. The Eldritch had a tentacle wrapped around Popeye's neck, swirling in a circle, choking him. Meanwhile, it slithered a tentacle around each of his extremities, drawing and quartering him.

The one-eyed sailor howled. Olive wailed.

I fell to my knees and hoped I remembered the incantation to put the thing back to sleep.

Prayer for the Dying

7:06 PM – DAY 3

A merry mix of grunts, groans, clicks, squeals, and sobs filled the air. The Eldritch stretched Popeye. I didn't know how much more the sailor's limbs could take before they snapped off.

I closed my eyes and pulled up the picture of The Eldritch incantation I needed. Popeye screamed. Olive howled. The Eldritch clicked its beaks.

The words came easy. I heard Artie saying them in my head and I just parroted them. At once, the Old One froze. Its grip on Popeye weakened, but the creature did not release him. The Eldritch fixed an eye on me. Popeye went to speak, but a tentacle slid over his mouth.

I opened my eyes and repeated the incantation, and then again. The Eldritch withdrew its tentacles. Popeye crashed to the ground with a thud and a grumble. The walls stopped bending as the things on the other side backed off.

A small green light flashed deep inside the ancient god, growing in intensity with every pulse until it blinded. The Old One stumbled in place, then fell onto its side. A tentacle slithered out in front of it, grabbing onto the ground. The monster dragged itself forward, towards the sea, but went still and limp after it traveled a foot or two. The glow behind its eyes dimmed, and then The Eldritch drifted off to sleep. Its eyes closed and the creatures on the other side retreated to the darkness or whatever space they resided.

I repeated the incantation two more times for good measure.

Popeye rose to his feet and gave me a nod, which I returned.

The cultists filed out of the cannery, returning to their homes in Sweethaven. Arkham's best tore into the dark and I lost sight of them as they vanished into the fog.

The call and the spell broken... for today.

"Remember what I's said about explaining to Olive."

And then, he bolted through the loading dock and disappeared into the foggy night, a giant shadow among shadows.

I made my way downstairs and freed Olive from her bindings. She threw her arms around me and sobbed into my shoulder. I didn't know what to say to the dame, so I just patted her on the back.

I broke our embrace when I heard the beating of wings and the squawking of what sounded like a nightmarish bird. I turned in time to witness a vulture the size of a small boat swoop down and snatch the Sea Hag in its talons. The malformed bird of prey swung back its head to squawk at me before flying into the rainy, dark sky.

The *whoosh, whoosh* of its wings grew faint. A witch's cackle rose over it and echoed in the darkness.

Ain't No Sunshine

8:32 PM – DAY 3

I escorted Olive Oyl to her home. Despite the earlier excitement, Sweethaven had eased into a silent slumber. Olive pecked my cheek, then looked away.

"I'm sorry about Dollface, Detective. She was special."

"That she was, Miss Oyl."

We stood looking at each other in a moment of silence, in reverence for our fallen comrades. She turned and made for the door. I took my cue and hit the street.

"Thank you, Detective. For finding Popeye."

For once, the dame's voice didn't grate on me.

"No sweat, doll."

Behind me, Olive's door opened, then tapped shut.

Case closed.

Run Between the Raindrops

8:32 PM – DAY 3

The rain beat down on Sweethaven without mercy. Thanks to my fresh fins and fish-form, I didn't mind the rain so much. But I didn't enjoy it. I wondered if I would enjoy anything again. Without Dollface, my dark world grew even darker. I failed her, but rescued Sweethaven from cosmic horrors. Still, the scales tipped in the wrong direction for me.

I don't know how long I wandered in the rain, but somewhere between the cannery and the office, I stood in the middle of the street and danced.

And I almost enjoyed it.

Here's to you, Dollface, wherever you are.

We'll always have Sweethaven.

Epilogue: Night Watch

11:57 PM – Day 3

I sat behind my desk and poured myself a glass of moonshine. The place seemed both familiar and strange, like a favorite shirt you outgrew. I wondered if it was time to move on. Start fresh in a new space. These digs felt spooky, inhabited by more than mere man. Memories stained every floorboard and ceiling tile. Her face haunted me like Marley's ghost, minus the rattling cashboxes and keys.

Through the windows, I watched the rain fall and the green full moon travel across the sky. While so much appeared different, too much remained the same. The work is never done. The watch never ends.

A shadow appeared in the window. I caught its reflection moving in the dark corners of the office behind me. Its shape familiar.

"I think this belongs to you," Popeye said, throwing my crushed hat onto the desk.

"Oh, hey!"

I gaped at my hat as though it was my favorite childhood toy. I fluffed it back into shape and eased it onto my head. It wasn't a perfect fit, thanks to my new fish features, but it fit well enough.

"Drink?"

"Sure, why not?"

Popeye crashed into the couch. I hand-delivered the bottle of moonshine and plopped beside him. He pressed the bottle to his lips and took a drink.

"That's horrible!"

He grimaced, but took another drink. A longer one.

"Yeah. It is. But it's all they serve in this joint. We make do in Sweethaven."

I sat and drank with Popeye until I couldn't see the hands on the wall clock. The thought that this guy turned into a head-popping hulking beast shocked me, but then again, I wondered what havoc my darker half would wreak now that my change was complete. I noted my bat-like hearing had returned.

As what passed for morning in Sweethaven broke, the silence between us ended.

"Olive?"

I nodded.

"She understands, I think. She doesn't agree, but..."

"It's safer this way. If there's a way back to what I was... what we were..."

"She might have changed, too. You ever think of that?"

Popeye considered, then nodded.

"I'm a monster. Monsters live in the shadows. Alone."

"As you wish. Just... think about it, okay?"

Popeye said nothing, but I felt the angst drain.

"You know, we ain't seen the last of that Sea Hag. The cannery's for sale, or what's left of it. How long before a new player tries to fill the void left by the departed dons?"

Popeye downed the last of the moonshine.

"They're here already. Short, stocky guy with a thick beard. I didn't catch a name. We should keep an eye on him."

He dropped the empty bottle in my lap and got to his feet with ease, considering how much moonshine he drank.

"We?" I asked. "I'd raise an eyebrow if I still had any."

Fish don't have eyebrows.

Popeye skulked into the front room, blending with the darkness. The doorknob rattled and a slice of silver light spilled into the front room. The one-eyed sailor looked back at me.

"You need a partner, Detective. And I need... a friend."

"What about monsters being alone?"

"We're all monsters, Chase."

He slipped into the hall, closing the door behind him.

I took off my hat and kicked back onto the couch. The case... cases were closed, but the job wasn't done, not when Sweethaven remained behind an impenetrable wall of fog, trapped inside a living nightmare and a gang of Arkham's escaped lunatics lurked in the dark. And that was just for starters. Experience told me the worst was yet to come.

Our lives had changed, as well as our bodies. Somehow, we'd have to reconcile an ancient god sleeping in the sea, and a powerful sea witch bent on revenge and chaos. Gotta love Sweethaven.

I thought about getting Dollface's note out of the safe and reading it, but I let it be. I'd know when the time was right. There was still so much work to do in Sweethaven. It wasn't the seafaring town it used to be.

The Sea Hag would be back, and there were already new players coming out of the shadows to take the place of the fallen dons—not to mention the otherworldly creatures that were only for today kept at bay. The Old Gods are called that because they only go away for a while, but they always come back. You can't kill a God.

I decided one day, when the work was done and I hung up my hat for good, then and only then would I sit behind my desk, pour myself a drink, raise a glass to the best gal Friday that there ever was, and read Dollface's letter.

One day seemed so far away...

The dame would understand the delay. She always did, better than me.

Tomorrow, the night watch began. I had new memories to make to replace the ones lost.

Today, I closed my eyes and covered my face with my hat. I listened to the rain on the windows until I slipped into sleep. It always rains in Sweethaven. You notice that?

Ah, maybe someday I'll make it out of Sweethaven—just not today.

That's my story. You can choose to believe it or not. It makes no difference to me. But before you scowl and tell me to brush off, I wanna ask you a question—

tell me...

do you dream much?

Twisted Tales of Familiar Faces

If you enjoyed this hair-raising retelling of the classic *Popeye*, don't miss out on the rest of this horrifying collection!

Humbug (Scrooge) - Andre Gonzalez

Sweethaven (Popeye) - RJ Clark

Timber Beast (Paul Bunyan) - A.K. Hughey

Alice (Alice in Wonderland) - Audrey Brice

Wish (Aladdin) - Courtney Konstantin

Quixote (Don Quixote) - Stephen Wertzbaugher

Arturius (King Arthur) - A.K. Hughey

Steamboat (Steamboat Willie) - Courtney Konstantin

Strangled (Rapunzel) - Stephen Wertzbaugher

Dethroning Oz (Wizard of Oz) - Audrey Brice

Scorned (Hercules) - Z.S. Diamanti

Check out the entire collection at www.m4lpublishing.com

Join our newsletter to stay up to date with all upcoming releases at www.m4lpublishing.com

Author's Note

I never could have written Sweethaven without reading the brilliant works of Dashiell Hammett, Elmore Leonard, Raymond Chandler, Walter Mosley, H.P. Lovecraft, Mickey Spillane, James Ellroy, and Stephen King.

I also never could have written it without the love and support of my partner-in-crime and in life, Dana Rose DeFrancesco. Thank you for your patience, and always pushing me forward.

Thanks also goes to:

My trusty alpha and beta readers — you know who you are!

Melissa Prideaux — for always making me sound better and smarter than I am!

Andre and Natasha Gonzalez — for your faith in me, again, and for letting me run with Popeye! It was such a blast!

And a final shout out to my loyal Staycation-ers and everyone who's come along with me on this wild ride! The best is yet to come!

RJ Clark

Asbury Park, NJ

November 2024

Enjoy this book?

We hope you enjoyed this release from M4L Publishing.

Reviews are the most helpful tools in getting new readers for any books. We don't have the financial backing of a New York publishing house and can't afford to blast our books on billboards or bus stops.

(Not yet!)

That said, your honest review can go a long way in helping us reach new readers. If you've enjoyed this book, we'd be forever grateful if you could spend a couple minutes leaving it a review (it can be as short as you like) on the site you purchased this book from.

Thank you so much!

About the author

RJ CLARK began his professional career as a child actor and model, following in his famous uncle's footsteps, Stanley Clements. RJ's face was seen nationwide in the U.S. Army "Stay in School" print ad campaign. He also appeared regularly on daytime television, and worked on numerous film and commercial projects before inevitably returning to his first true love, writing.

As a screenwriter, RJ's screenplays won first prize or placed in the top 5 of nearly every major national—and international—competition worth mentioning. His novella, Two for One launched the indie literary magazine "The Instagatorzine," broken into two parts across the magazine's first two issues.

A native New Yorker, RJ attended NYU, holds a BFA and an MFA. He has lived in all five boroughs, but now calls historic Asbury Park, NJ home with his wife and dog, an Aussillon named Venus.

While RJ no longer works in the theatre as an actor, he provides accessibility services for deaf patrons at live performances throughout the country. He is passionate about theatre being for all and enjoys being able to introduce new shows to deaf or hard-of-hearing patrons.

When not writing, you're most likely to find RJ either playing guitar along the Jersey Shore, taking photographs of cool dogs and musicians around Asbury Park, voraciously reading new books, working on new music, or traveling the world.

A few of RJ's most favorite things include black coffee, chocolate, Stephen King, peanut butter, Pringle's, Truman Capote, tabletop games, the Universal Studios Monsters, horror movies, and David Tennant.